STORIES AT THE SPEED OF LIFE

JAMES PATTERSON
BOOKSHOTS

The new, incredibly
suspenseful
ALEX CROSS—availa
only in BOOKSHOTS

CROSS
KIL

ERY
on, J.

$4.99 US / $5.99 CAN
ISBN 978-0-316-31714-6

9 780316 317146

50499

EAN

BOOK

SACRAMENTO PUBLIC LIBRARY
828 "I" STREET
SACRAMENTO, CA 95814
04/2017

AVAILABLE NOW!

CROSS KILL

Along Came a Spider killer Gary Soneji died years ago. But Alex Cross swears he sees Soneji gun down his partner. Is his greatest enemy back from the grave?

ZOO II

Humans are evolving into a savage new species that could save civilization—or end it. James Patterson's *Zoo* was just the beginning.

UPCOMING TITLES

THE TRIAL

An accused killer will do anything to disrupt his own trial, including a courtroom shocker that Lindsay Boxer and the Womens's Murder Club will never see coming.

LITTLE BLACK DRESS

Can a little black dress change everything? What begins as one woman's fantasy is about to go too far.

LET'S PLAY MAKE-BELIEVE

Christy and Marty just met, and it's love at first sight. Or is it? One of them is playing a dangerous game—and only one will survive.

CHASE

A man falls to his death in an apparent accident....But why does he have a dead man's fingerprints? Detective Michael Bennett is on the case.

HUNTED

Someone is luring men from the streets to play a mysterious high-stakes game. Former Special Forces officer David Shelley goes undercover to shut it down—but will he win?

$10,000,000 MARRIAGE PROPOSAL

A mysterious billboard offering $10 million to get married intrigues three single women in LA. But who is Mr. Right…and is he the perfect match for the lucky winner?

THE FRENCH KISS

It's hard enough to move to a new city, but now everyone French detective Luc Moncrief cares about is being killed off. Welcome to New York.

KILLER CHEF

Caleb Rooney knows how to do two things: run a food truck and solve a murder. When people suddenly start dying of foodborne illnesses, the stakes are higher than ever….

113 MINUTES

Molly Rourke's son has been murdered. Now she'll do whatever it takes to get justice. No one should underestimate a mother's love….

THE CHRISTMAS MYSTERY

Two stolen paintings disappear from a Park Avenue murder scene—French detective Luc Moncrief is in for a merry Christmas.

BLACK & BLUE

Detective Harry Blue is determined to take down the serial killer who's abducted several women, but her mission leads to a shocking revelation.

James Patterson's
BOOKSHOTS
Flames

UPCOMING ROMANCES

LEARNING TO RIDE

City girl Madeline Harper never wanted to love a cowboy. But rodeo king Tanner Callen might change her mind…and win her heart.

THE McCULLAGH INN IN MAINE

Chelsea O'Kane escapes to Maine to build a new life—until she runs into Jeremy Holland, an old flame….

SACKING THE QUARTERBACK

Attorney Melissa St. James wins every case. Now, when she's defending football superstar Grayson Knight, her heart is on the line too.

DAZZLING: THE DIAMOND TRILOGY, PART I

To support her artistic career, Siobhan works at the elite Stone Room in New York City…never expecting to be swept away by Derick Miller.

RADIANT: THE DIAMOND TRILOGY, PART II

After an explosive breakup with her billionaire boyfriend, Siobhan moves to Detroit to pursue her art. But Derick isn't ready to give her up.

BODYGUARD

Special Agent Abbie Whitmore has only one task: protect Congressman Jonathan Lassiter from a violent cartel's threats. Yet she's never had to do it while falling in love….

WILL THE LAST HUMANS ON EARTH PLEASE TURN OUT THE LIGHTS?

As humans continue to be plagued by vicious animal attacks, zoologist Jackson Oz desperately tries to save the ones he loves— and the rest of mankind. But animals aren't the only threat anymore. Some *humans* are starting to evolve too, turning into something feral and ferocious....

Could this savage new species save civilization—or end it?

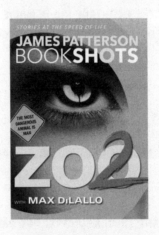

READ THE HIGH-ADRENALINE PAGE-TURNER **ZOO II**,

AVAILABLE ONLY FROM

BOOK**SHOTS**

CROSS KILL

JAMES PATTERSON

BOOK**SHOTS**

Little, Brown and Company

New York Boston London

The characters and events in this book are fictitious. Any similarity to real persons, living or dead, is coincidental and not intended by the author.

Copyright © 2016 by James Patterson

Hachette Book Group supports the right to free expression and the value of copyright. The purpose of copyright is to encourage writers and artists to produce the creative works that enrich our culture.

The scanning, uploading, and distribution of this book without permission is a theft of the author's intellectual property. If you would like permission to use material from the book (other than for review purposes), please contact permissions@hbgusa.com. Thank you for your support of the author's rights.

BookShots / Little, Brown and Company
Hachette Book Group
1290 Avenue of the Americas, New York, NY 10104
bookshots.com

First Edition: June 2016

BookShots is an imprint of Little, Brown and Company, a division of Hachette Book Group, Inc. The Little, Brown name and logo are trademarks of Hachette Book Group, Inc. The BookShots name and logo are a trademark of JBP Business, LLC.

The publisher is not responsible for websites (or their content) that are not owned by the publisher.

The Hachette Speakers Bureau provides a wide range of authors for speaking events. To find out more, go to hachettespeakersbureau.com or call (866) 376-6591.

ISBN 978-0-316-31714-6
LCCN 2016934160

10 9 8 7 6 5 4 3 2 1

RRD-C

Printed in the United States of America

CROSS KILL

CHAPTER 1

A LATE WINTER STORM bore down on Washington, DC, that March morning, and more folks than usual were waiting in the cafeteria of St. Anthony of Padua Catholic School on Monroe Avenue in the northeast quadrant.

"If you need a jolt before you eat, coffee's in those urns over there," I called to the cafeteria line.

From behind a serving counter, my partner, John Sampson, said, "You want pancakes or eggs and sausage, you come see me first. Dry cereal, oatmeal, and toast at the end. Fruit, too."

It was early, a quarter to seven, and we'd already seen twenty-five people come through the kitchen, mostly moms and kids from the surrounding neighborhood. By my count, another forty were waiting in the hallway, with more coming in from outside where the first flakes were falling.

It was all my ninety-something grandmother's idea. She'd hit the DC Lottery Powerball the year before, and wanted to make sure the unfortunate received some of her good fortune. She'd partnered with the church to see the hot-breakfast program started.

"Are there any doughnuts?" asked a little boy, who put me in mind of my younger son, Ali.

He was holding on to his mother, a devastatingly thin woman with rheumy eyes and a habit of scratching at her neck.

"No doughnuts today," I said.

"What am I gonna eat?" he complained.

"Something that's good for you for once," his mom said. "Eggs, bacon, and toast. Not all that Cocoa Puffs sugar crap."

I nodded. Mom looked like she was high on something, but she did know her nutrition.

"This sucks," her son said. "I want a doughnut. I want two doughnuts!"

"Go on, there," his mom said, and pushed him toward Sampson.

"Kind of overkill for a church cafeteria," said the man who followed her. He was in his late twenties, and dressed in baggy jeans, Timberland boots, and a big gray snorkel jacket.

I realized he was talking to me and looked at him, puzzled.

"Bulletproof vest?" he said.

"Oh," I said, and shrugged at the body armor beneath my shirt.

Sampson and I are major case detectives with the Washington, DC, Metropolitan Police Department. Immediately after our shift in the soup kitchen, we were joining a team taking down a drug gang operating in the streets around St. Anthony's. Members of the gang had been known to take free breakfasts at the school from time to time, so we'd decided to armor up. Just in case.

I wasn't telling him that, though. I couldn't identify him as a known gangster, but he looked the part.

"I'm up for a PT test end of next week," I said. "Got to get used to the weight since I'll be running three miles with it on."

"That vest make you hotter or colder today?"

"Warmer. Always."

"I need one of them," he said, and shivered. "I'm from Miami, you know? I must have been crazy to want to come on up here."

"Why did you come up here?" I asked.

"School. I'm a freshman at Howard."

"You're not on the meal program?"

"Barely making my tuition."

I saw him in a whole new light then, and was about to say so when gunshots rang out and people began to scream.

CHAPTER 2

DRAWING MY SERVICE PISTOL, I pushed against the fleeing crowd, hearing two more shots, and realizing they were coming from inside the kitchen behind Sampson. My partner had figured it out as well.

Sampson spun away from the eggs and bacon, drew his gun as I vaulted over the counter. We split and went to either side of the pair of swinging industrial kitchen doors. There were small portholes in both.

Ignoring the people still bolting from the cafeteria, I leaned forward and took a quick peek. Mixing bowls had spilled off the stainless-steel counters, throwing flour and eggs across the cement floor. Nothing moved, and I could detect no one inside.

Sampson took a longer look from the opposite angle. His face almost immediately screwed up.

"Two wounded," he hissed. "The cook, Theresa, and a nun I've never seen before."

"How bad?"

"There's blood all over Theresa's white apron. Looks like the nun's hit in the leg. She's sitting up against the stove with a big pool below her."

"Femoral?"

Sampson took another look and said, "It's a lot of blood."

"Cover me," I said. "I'm going in low to get them."

Sampson nodded. I squatted down and threw my shoulder into the door, which swung away. Half expecting some unseen gunman to open fire, I rolled inside. I slid through the slurry of two dozen eggs, and came to a stop on the floor between two prep counters.

Sampson came in with his weapon high, searching for a target.

But no one shot. No one moved. And there was no sound except the labored breathing of the cook and the nun who were to our left, on the other side of a counter, by a big industrial stove.

The nun's eyes were open and bewildered. The cook's head slumped but she was breathing.

I scrambled under the prep counter to the women, and started tugging off my belt. The nun shrank from me when I reached for her.

"I'm a cop, Sister," I said. "My name is Alex Cross. I need to put a tourniquet on your leg or you could die."

She blinked, but then nodded.

"John?" I said, observing a serious gunshot wound to her lower thigh. A needle-thin jet of blood erupted with every heartbeat.

"Right here," Sampson said behind me. "Just seeing what's what."

"Call it in," I said, as I wrapped the belt around her upper thigh, cinching it tight. "We need two ambulances. Fast."

The blood stopped squirting. I could hear my partner making the radio call.

The nun's eyes fluttered and drifted toward shut.

"Sister," I said. "What happened? Who shot you?"

Her eyes blinked open. She gaped at me, disoriented for a moment, before her attention strayed past me. Her eyes widened, and the skin of her cheek went taut with terror.

I snatched up my gun and spun around, raising the pistol. I saw Sampson with his back to me, radio to his ear, gun lowered, and then a door at the back of the kitchen. It had swung open, revealing a large pantry.

A man crouched in a fighting stance in the pantry doorway.

In his crossed arms he held two nickel-plated pistols, one aimed at Sampson and the other at me.

With all the training I've been lucky enough to receive over the years, you'd think I would have done the instinctual thing for a veteran cop facing an armed assailant, that I would have registered *Man with gun!* in my brain, and I would have shot him immediately.

But for a split second I didn't listen to *Man with a gun!* because I was too stunned by the fact that I knew him, and that he was long, long dead.

CHAPTER 3

IN THAT SAME INSTANT, he fired both pistols. Traveling less than thirty feet, the bullet hit me so hard it slammed me backward. My head cracked off the concrete and everything went just this side of midnight, like I was swirling and draining down a black pipe, before I heard a third shot and then a fourth.

Something crashed close to me, and I fought my way toward the sound, toward consciousness, seeing the blackness give way, disjointed and incomplete, like a jigsaw puzzle with missing pieces.

Five, maybe six seconds passed before I found more pieces, and I knew who I was and what had happened. Two more seconds passed before I realized I'd taken the bullet square in the Kevlar that covered my chest. It felt like I'd taken a sledgehammer to my ribs, and a swift kick to my head.

In the next instant, I grabbed my gun and looked for…

John Sampson sprawled on the floor by the sinks, his massive frame looking crumpled until he started twitching electrically, and I saw the head wound.

"No," I shouted, becoming fully alert, and stumbling over to his side.

Sampson's eyes were rolled up in his head and quivering. I grabbed the radio on the floor beyond him, hit the transmitter, and said, "This is Detective Alex Cross. Ten-Zero-Zero. Repeat. Officer down. Monroe Avenue and 12th, Northeast. St. Anthony's Catholic School kitchen. Multiple shots fired. Ten-Fifty-Twos needed immediately. Repeat. Multiple ambulances needed, and a Life Flight for officer with head wound!"

"We have ambulances and patrols on their way, Detective," the dispatcher came back. "ETA twenty seconds. I'll call Life Flight. Do you have the shooter?"

"No, damn it. Make the Life Flight call."

The line went dead. I lowered the radio. Only then did I look back at the best friend I've ever had, the first kid I met after Nana Mama brought me up from South Carolina, the man I'd grown up with, the partner I'd relied on more times than I could count. The spasms subsided and Sampson's eyes lolled and he gasped.

"John," I said, kneeling beside him and taking his hand. "Hold on now. Cavalry's coming."

He seemed not to hear, just stared vacantly past me toward the wall.

I started to cry. I couldn't stop. I shook from head to toe, and then I wanted to shoot the man who'd done this. I wanted to shoot him twenty times, completely destroy the creature that had risen from the dead.

Sirens closed in on the school from six directions. I wiped at my tears, and then squeezed Sampson's hand, before forcing myself to my feet and back out into the cafeteria, where the first patrol officers were charging in, followed by a pair of EMTs whose shoulders were flecked with melting snowflakes.

They got Sampson's head immobilized, then put him on a board and then a gurney. He was under blankets and moving in less than six minutes. It was snowing hard outside. They waited inside the front door to the school for the helicopter to come, and put IV lines into his wrists.

Sampson went into another convulsion. The parish priest, Father Fred Close, came and gave my partner the last rites.

But my man was still hanging on when the helicopter came. In a daze I followed them out into a driving snowstorm. We had to shield our eyes to duck under the blinding propeller wash and get Sampson aboard.

"We'll take it from here!" one EMT shouted at me.

"There's not a chance I'm leaving his side," I said, climbed in beside the pilot, and pulled on the extra helmet. "Let's go."

The pilot waited until they had the rear doors shut and the gurney strapped down before throttling up the helicopter. We began to rise, and it was only then that I saw through the swirling snow that crowds were forming beyond the barricades set up in a perimeter around the school and church complex.

We pivoted in the air and flew back up over 12th Street, rising above the crowd. I looked down through the spiraling snow and saw everyone ducking their heads from the helicopter wash. Everyone except for a single male face looking directly up at the Life Flight, not caring about the battering, stinging snow.

"That's him!" I said.

"Detective?" the pilot said, his voice crackling over the radio in my helmet.

I tugged down the microphone, and said, "How do I talk to dispatch?"

The pilot leaned over, and flipped a switch.

"This is Detective Alex Cross," I said. "Who's the supervising detective heading to St. Anthony's?"

"Your wife. Chief Stone."

"Patch me through to her."

Five seconds passed as we built speed and hurtled toward the hospital.

"Alex?" Bree said. "What's happened?"

"John's hit bad, Bree," I said. "I'm with him. Close off that school from four blocks in every direction. Order a door-to-door search. I just saw the shooter on 12th, a block west of the school."

"Description?"

"It's Gary Soneji, Bree," I said. "Get his picture off Google and send it to every cop in the area."

There was silence on the line before Bree said sympathetically, "Alex, are *you* okay? Gary Soneji's been dead for years."

"If he's dead, then I just saw a ghost."

CHAPTER 4

WE WERE BUFFETED BY winds and faced near-whiteout conditions trying to land on the helipad atop George Washington Medical Center. In the end we put down in the parking lot by the ER entrance, where a team of nurses and doctors met us.

They hustled Sampson inside and got him attached to monitors while Dr. Christopher Kalhorn, a neurosurgeon, swabbed aside some of the blood and examined the head wounds.

The bullet had entered Sampson's skull at a shallow angle about two inches above the bridge of his nose. It exited forward of his left temple. That second wound was about the size of a marble, but gaping and ragged, as if the bullet had been a hollow point that broke up and shattered going through bone.

"Let's get him intubated, on Propofol, and into an ice bath and cooling helmet," Kalhorn said. "Take his temp down to ninety-two, get him into a CT scanner, and then the OR. I'll have a team waiting for him."

The ER doctors and nurses sprang into action. In short order, they had a breathing tube down Sampson's throat and were racing him away. Kalhorn turned to leave. I showed my badge and stopped him.

"That's my brother," I said. "What do I tell his wife?"

Dr. Kalhorn turned grim. "You tell her we'll do everything possible to save him. And you tell her to pray. You, too, Detective."

"What are his chances?"

"Pray," he said, took off in a trot, and disappeared.

I was left standing in an empty treatment slot in the ER, looking down at the dark blood that stained the gauze pads they'd used to clean Sampson's head.

"You can't stay in here, Detective," one of the nurses said sympathetically. "We need the space. Traffic accidents all over the city with this storm."

I nodded, turned, and wandered away, wondering where to go, what to do.

I went out in the ER waiting area and saw twenty people in the seats. They stared at my pistol, at the blood on my shirt, and at the black hole where Soneji's bullet had hit me. I didn't care what they thought. I didn't—

I heard the automatic doors *whoosh* open behind me.

A fearful voice cried out, "Alex?"

I swung around. Billie Sampson was standing there in pink hospital scrub pants and a down coat, shaking from head to toe from the cold and the threat of something far more bitter. "How bad is it?"

Billie's a surgical nurse, so there was no point in being vague. I described the wound. Her hand flew to her mouth at first, but then she shook her head. "It's bad. He's lucky to be alive."

I hugged her and said, "He's a strong man. But he's going to need your prayers. He's going to need all our prayers."

Billie's strength gave way. She began to moan and sob into my chest, and I held her tighter. When I raised my head, the people in the waiting room were looking on in concern.

"Let's get out of here," I muttered, and led Billie out into the hallway and to the chapel.

We went inside, and thankfully it was empty. I got Billie calmed down enough to tell her what had happened at the school and afterward.

"They've put him into a chemical coma and are supercooling his body."

"To reduce swelling and bleeding," she said, nodding.

"And the neurosurgeons here are the best. He's in their hands now."

"And God's," Billie said, staring at the cross on the wall in the chapel before pulling away from me to go down on her knees.

I joined her and we held hands and begged our savior for mercy.

CHAPTER 5

HOURS PASSED LIKE DAYS as we waited outside the surgical unit. Bree showed up before noon.

"Anything?" she asked.

I shook my head.

"Billie," Bree said, hugging her. "We're going to find who did this to John. I promise you that."

"You didn't find Soneji?" I asked in disbelief. "How could he have gotten away if you'd cordoned off the area?"

My wife looked over at me, studied me. "Soneji's dead, Alex. You all but killed him yourself."

My mouth hung open, and I blinked several times. "You mean you didn't send his picture out? You didn't look for him?"

"We looked for someone who looked like Soneji," Bree said defensively.

"No," I said. "He was less than thirty feet from me, light shining down on his face. It was him."

"Then explain how a man who all but disintegrated right before your eyes can surface more than a decade later," Bree said.

"I can't explain it," I said. "I…maybe I need some coffee. Want some?"

They shook their heads, and I got up, heading toward the hospital cafeteria, seeing flashbacks from long ago.

I put Gary Soneji in prison after he went on a kidnapping and murder spree that threatened my family. Soneji escaped several years later, and turned to bomb building. He detonated several, killing multiple people before we spotted him in New York City. We chased Soneji into Grand Central Station, where we feared he'd explode another bomb. Instead he grabbed a baby.

At one point, Soneji held the baby up and screamed at me, "This doesn't end here, Cross. I'm coming for you, even from the grave if I have to."

Then he threw the infant at us. Someone caught her, but Soneji escaped into the vast abandoned tunnel system below Manhattan. We tracked him in there. Soneji attacked me in the darkness, and knocked me down and almost killed me before I was able to shoot him. The bullet shattered his jaw, ripped apart his tongue, and blew out the side of one cheek.

Soneji staggered away from me, was swallowed by the darkness. He must have pitched forward then and sprawled on the rocky tunnel floor. The impact set off a small bomb in his pocket. The tunnel exploded into white-hot flames.

When I got to him, Soneji was engulfed, curled up, and screaming. It lasted several seconds before he stopped. I stood there and watched Soneji burn. I saw him shrivel up and turn coal black.

But as sure as I was of that memory, I was also sure I'd seen Gary

Soneji that morning, a split second before he tried to shoot me in the heart and blow Sampson's head off.

I'm coming for you, even from the grave if I have to.

Soneji's taunt echoed back to me after I'd gotten my coffee.

After several sips, I decided I had to assume Soneji was still dead. So I'd seen, what, a double? An impostor?

I supposed it was possible with plastic surgery, but the likeness had been so dead-on, from the thin reddish mustache to the wispy hair to the crazed, amused expression.

It was him, I thought. *But how?*

This doesn't end here, Cross.

I saw Soneji so clearly then that I feared for my sanity.

This doesn't end here, Cross.

I'm coming for you, even from the grave if I have to.

CHAPTER 6

"ALEX?"

I startled, almost dropped my coffee, and saw Bree trotting down the hall toward me with a wary expression.

"He made it through the operation," she said. "He's in intensive care, and the doctor's going to talk to Billie in a few moments."

We both held Billie's hands when Dr. Kalhorn finally emerged. He looked drained.

"How is he?" Billie asked, after introducing herself.

"Your husband's a remarkable fighter," Kalhorn said. "He died once on the table, but rallied. Besides the trauma of the bullet, there were bone and bullet fragments we had to deal with. Three quarters of an inch left and one of those fragments would have caught a major artery, and we'd be having a different conversation."

"So he's going to live?" Billie asked.

"I can't promise you that," Kalhorn said. "The next forty-eight to seventy-two hours will be the most critical time for him. He's sustained a massive head injury, severe trauma to his upper-left temporal lobe. For now, we're keeping him in a medically induced coma, and we will keep him that way until we see a significant drop in brain swelling."

"If he comes out, what's the prognosis, given the extent of the injury you saw?" I asked.

"I can't tell you who he'll be if and when he wakes up," the neurosurgeon said. "That's up to God."

"Can we see him?" Bree asked.

"Give it a half hour," Kalhorn said. "There's a whirlwind around him at the moment. Lots of good people supporting him."

"Thank you, Doctor," Billie said, trying not to cry again. "For saving him."

"It was an honor," Kalhorn said, patted her on the arm, and smiled at Bree and me before returning to the ICU.

"Damage to his upper-left temporal lobe," Billie said.

"He's alive," I said. "Let's keep focused on that. Anything else, we'll deal with down the road."

Bree held her hand and said, "Alex is right. We've prayed him through surgery, and now we'll pray he wakes up."

But Billie still appeared uncertain forty minutes later when we donned surgical masks, gloves, and smocks and entered the room where Sampson lay.

You could barely see the slits of his eyes for the swelling. His head was wrapped in a turban of gauze, and there were so many tubes going into him, and so many monitors and devices beeping and clicking around him, that from the waist up he looked more machine than man.

"Oh, Jesus, John," Billie said when she got to his side. "What have they done to you?"

Bree rubbed Billie's back as tears wracked her again. I stayed only a few minutes, until I couldn't take seeing Sampson like that anymore.

"I'll be back," I told them. "Tonight before I go home to sleep."

"Where are you going?" Bree asked.

"To hunt Soneji," I said. "It's what John would want."

"There's a blizzard outside," Bree said. "And Internal Affairs is going to want to hear your report on the shooting."

"I don't give a damn about IA right now," I said, walking toward the door. "And a blizzard's exactly the kind of chaotic situation that Gary Soneji lives for."

Bree wasn't happy, but sighed and gestured to a shopping bag she'd brought with her. "You'll need your coat, hat, and gloves if you're going Soneji-hunting."

CHAPTER 7

OUTSIDE A BLIZZARD WAILED, a classic nor'easter with driving wet snow that was already eight inches deep. It takes only four inches to snarl Washington, DC, so completely that there's talk of bringing in the National Guard.

Georgetown was a parking lot. I trudged to the Foggy Bottom Metro station, ignoring my freezing-cold feet, and reliving old times with big John Sampson. I met him within days of moving up to DC with my brothers after my mother died and my father, her killer, disappeared, presumed dead.

John lived with his mother and sister. His father had died in Vietnam. We were in the same fifth-grade class. He was ten years old and big, even then. But so was I.

It made for a natural rivalry, and we didn't much care for each other at first. I was faster than him, which he did not like. He was stronger than me, which I did not like. The inevitable fight we had was a draw.

We were suspended for three days for fighting. Nana Mama marched me down to Sampson's house to apologize to him and to his mother for throwing the first punch.

I went unhappily. When Sampson came to the door equally annoyed, I saw the split lip and bruising around his right cheek and smiled. He saw the swelling around both of my eyes and smiled back.

We'd both inflicted damage. We both had won. And that was that. End of the war, and start of the longest friendship of my life.

I took the Metro across town, and walked back to St. Anthony's in the snow, trying to will myself not to remember Sampson in the ICU, more machine than man. But the image kept returning, and every time it did, I felt weaker, as if a part of me were dying.

There were still Metro police cars parked in front of the school, and two television trucks. I pulled the wool hat down and turned up the collar of my jacket. I didn't want to talk to any reporters about this case. Ever.

I showed my badge to the patrolman standing inside the front door, and started back toward the cafeteria and kitchen.

Father Close appeared at his office door. He recognized me.

"Your partner?"

"There's brain damage, but he's alive," I said.

"Another miracle, then," Father Close said. "Sister Mary Elliott and Theresa Ball, the cook, they're still alive as well. You saved them, Dr. Cross. If you hadn't been there, I fear all three of them would be dead."

"I don't think that's true," I said. "But thank you for saying so."

"Any idea when I can have my cafeteria and kitchen back?"

"I'll ask the crime-scene specialists, but figure tomorrow your students bring a bag lunch and eat in their homerooms. When it's a cop-involved shooting, the forensics folks are sticklers for detail."

"As they should be," Father Close said, thanked me again, and returned to his office.

I returned to the cafeteria and stood there a moment in the empty space, hearing voices in the kitchen, but recalling the first shots and how I'd reacted.

I went to the swinging industrial doors and did the same. We'd done it by the book, I decided, and pushed through them again.

I glanced at where the cook and nun had lain wounded, and then over where Sampson had lain dying before turning my attention to the pantry. This was where the book had been thrown out. In retrospect, we should have cleared the rest of the building before tending to the wounded. But it looked like femoral blood and…

Three crime-scene techs were still at work in the kitchen. Barbara Hatfield, an old friend, was in the pantry. She spotted me and came right over.

"How's John, Alex?"

"Hanging on," I said.

"Everyone's shaken up," Hatfield said. "And there's something you should see, something I was going to call you about later."

She led me into the pantry, floor-to-ceiling shelves loaded with foodstuffs and kitchen supplies, and a big shiny commercial freezer at the far end.

The words spray-painted in two lines across the face of the fridge stopped me dead in my tracks.

"Right?" Hatfield said. "I did the same thing."

CHAPTER 8

I WAS UP AT four o'clock the following morning, snuck out of bed without waking Bree, and on three hours of sleep went back to doing what I'd been doing. I got a cup of coffee and went up to the third floor, to my home office, where I had been going through my files on Gary Soneji.

I keep files on all the bad ones, but Soneji had the thickest file, six of them, in fact, all bulging. I'd left off at one in the morning with notes taken midway through the kidnapping of the US secretary of the treasury's son, and the daughter of a famous actress.

I tried to focus, tried to re-master the details. But I yawned after two paragraphs, drank coffee, and thought of John Sampson.

But only briefly. I decided that sitting by his side helped him little. I was better off looking for the man who put a bullet through John's head. So I read and reread, and noted dangling threads, abandoned lines of inquiry that Sampson and I had followed over the years but which had led nowhere.

After an hour, I found an old genealogy chart we and the US marshals put together on Soneji's family after he escaped prison.

Scanning it, I realized we'd let the marshals handle the pure fugitive hunt. I saw several names and relations I'd never talked to before, and wrote them down.

I ran their names through Google, and saw that two of them were still living at the addresses noted on the chart. How long had it been? Thirteen, fourteen years?

Then again, Nana Mama and I had lived in our house on 5th for more than thirty years. Americans do put down roots once in a while.

I glanced at my watch, saw it was past five, and wondered when I could try to make a few calls. No, I thought then, this kind of thing is best done in person. But the storm. I went to the window in the dormer of the office, pushed it up, and looked outside.

To my surprise, it was pouring rain and considerably warmer. Most of the snow was gone. That sealed it. I was going for a drive as soon as it was light enough to see.

Returning to my desk, I thought about going back downstairs to take a shower, but feared waking Bree. Her job as Metro's chief of detectives was stressful enough without dealing with the additional pressure of a cop shooting.

I tried to go back to the Soneji files, but instead called up a picture on my computer. I'd taken it the afternoon before. It showed the fridge and the spray-painted words the shooter had left behind.

CROSS KILL
Long Live Soneji!

I had obviously been the target. And why not? Soneji hated me as much as I hated him.

Had Soneji expected Sampson to be with me? The two pistols he'd fired said yes. I closed my eyes and saw him there in the doorway, arms crossed, left gun aimed at me, right gun at Sampson.

Something bothered me. I turned back to the file, rummaged around until I confirmed my memory. Soneji was left-handed, which explained why he'd crossed his arms to shoot. He was aiming at me with his better hand. He'd wanted me dead no matter what happened to John.

It was why Soneji shot for center of mass, I decided, and wondered whether his shot at Sampson was misaimed, if he'd clipped John's head in error.

Left-handed. It had to be Soneji. But it couldn't be Soneji.

In frustration, I shut the computer off, grabbed my notes, and snuck back into the bedroom. I shut the bathroom door without making a peep. After showering and dressing, I tried to get out light-footed, but made a floorboard squeak.

"I'm up, quiet as a mouse," Bree said.

"I'm going to New Jersey," I said.

"What?" she said, sitting up in bed and turning on the light. "Why?"

"To talk to some of Soneji's relatives, see if he's been in touch."

Bree shook her head. "He's dead, Alex."

"But what if the explosion I saw in the tunnel was *caused* by Soneji as he went by some bum living down there?" I said. "What if I didn't see Soneji burn?"

"You never did DNA on the remains?"

"There was no need. I saw him die. I identified him, so no one checked."

"Jesus, Alex," Bree said. "Is that possible? What did the shooter's face look like?"

"Like Soneji's," I said, frustrated.

"Well, did his jaw look like Soneji's? His tongue? Did he say anything?"

"He didn't say a word, but his face?" I frowned and thought about that. "I don't know."

"You said the light was good. You said you saw him clearly."

Was the light that good? Feeling a little wobbly, I nevertheless closed my eyes, trying to bring more of the memory back and into sharper focus.

I saw Soneji standing there in the pantry doorway, arms crossed, chin tucked, and…looking directly at me. He shot at Sampson without even aiming. It *was* me he'd wanted to kill.

What about his jaw? I replayed memory again and again before I saw it.

"There was something there," I said, running my fingers along my left jawline.

"A shadow?" Bree said.

I shook my head. "More like a scar."

CHAPTER 9

THREE HOURS LATER, I'D left I-95 for Route 29, which parallels the Delaware River. Heading upstream, I soon realized that I was not far from East Amwell Township, where the aviator Charles Lindbergh's baby was kidnapped in 1932.

Gary Soneji had been obsessed with the Lindbergh case. He'd studied it in preparing for the kidnappings of the treasury secretary's son, the late Michael Goldberg, and Maggie Rose Dunne, the daughter of a famous actress.

I'd noticed before on a map the proximity of East Amwell to Rosemont, where Soneji grew up. But it wasn't until I pulled through the tiny unincorporated settlement that I realized Soneji had spent his early life less than five miles from the Lindbergh kidnapping site.

Rosemont itself was quaint and leafy, with rock walls giving way to sopping green fields.

I tried to imagine Soneji as a boy in this rural setting, tried to see him discovering the crime of the century. He wouldn't have cared much for the police detectives who'd worked the

Lindbergh case. No, Soneji would have obsessed on the information surrounding Bruno Hauptmann, the career criminal convicted and executed for taking the toddler and caving in his skull.

My mind was flooded with memories of going into Soneji's apartment for the first time, seeing what was essentially a shrine to Hauptmann and the Lindbergh case. In writings we found back then, Soneji had fantasized about being Hauptmann in the days just before the killer was caught, when the whole world was fixated and speculating on the mystery he'd set in motion.

"Audacious criminals change history," Soneji wrote. "Audacious criminals are remembered long after they're gone, which is more than can be said of the detectives who chase them."

I found the address on the Rosemont Ringoes Road, and pulled over on the shoulder beyond the drive. The storm had ebbed to sprinkles when I climbed out in front of a gray-and-white clapboard cottage set back in pines.

The yard was sparse and littered with wet pine needles. The front stoop was cracked and listed to one side, so I had to hold on to the iron railing in order to ring the bell.

A few moments later, one of the curtains fluttered. A few moments after that, the door swung open, revealing a bald man in his seventies. He leaned over a walker and had an oxygen line running into his nose.

"Peter Soneji?"

"What do you want?"

"I'm Alex Cross. I'm a—"

"I know who you are," Gary Soneji's father snapped icily. "My son's killer."

"He blew himself up."

"So you've said."

"Can I talk to you, sir?"

"Sir?" Peter Soneji said and laughed caustically. "Now it's 'sir'"?

"Far as I know, you never had anything to do with your son's criminal career," I said.

"Tell that to the reporters who've shown up at my door over the years," Soneji's father said. "The things they've accused me of. Father to a monster."

"I'm not accusing you of anything, *Mr. Soneji*," I said. "I'm simply looking for your take on a few loose ends."

"With everything on the internet about Gary, you'd think there'd be no loose ends."

"These are questions from my personal files," I said.

Soneji's father gave me a long, considered look before saying, "Leave it alone, Detective. Gary's long dead. Far as I'm concerned, good riddance."

He tried to shut the door in my face, but I stopped him.

"I can call the sheriff," Peter Soneji protested.

"Just one question and then I'll leave," I said. "How did Gary become obsessed with the Lindbergh kidnapping?"

CHAPTER 10

TWO HOURS LATER AS I drove through the outskirts of Crumpton, Maryland, I was still wrestling with the answer Soneji's father had given me. It seemed to offer new insight into his son, but I still couldn't explain how or why yet.

I found the second address. The farmhouse had once been a cheery yellow, but the paint was peeling and streaked with dark mold. Every window was encased in the kind of iron barring you see in big cities.

As I walked across the front yard toward the porch, I stirred up several pigeons, flushing them from the dead weeds. I heard a weird voice talking somewhere behind the house.

The porch was dominated by several old machine tools, lathes and such, that I had to step around in order to knock at a steel door with triple dead bolts.

I knocked a second time, and was thinking I should go around the house where I'd heard the odd voice. But then the dead bolts were thrown one by one.

The door opened, revealing a dark-haired woman in her forties, with a sharp nose and dull brown eyes. She wore a grease-stained one-piece Carhartt canvas coverall, and carried at port arms an AR-style rifle with a big banana clip.

"Salesman, you are standing on my property uninvited," she said. "I have ample cause to shoot you where you stand."

I showed her my badge and ID, said, "I'm not a salesman. I'm a cop. I should have called ahead, but I didn't have a number."

Instead of calming her down, that only got her more agitated. "What are the police doing at sweet Ginny Winslow's door? Looking to persecute a gun lover?"

"I just want to ask you a few questions, Mrs. Soneji," I said.

Soneji's widow flinched at the name, and turned spitting mad. "My name's been legally changed to Virginia Winslow going on seven years now, and I still can't get the stench of Gary off my skin. What's your name? Who are you with?"

"Alex Cross," I said. "With DC…"

She hardened, said, "I know you now. I remember you from TV."

"Yes, ma'am."

"You never came to talk with me. Just them US marshals. Like I didn't even exist."

"I'm here to talk now," I said.

"Ten years too late. Get the hell off my property before I embrace my Second Amendment rights and—"

"I saw Gary's father this morning," I said. "He told me how Gary's obsession with the Lindbergh kidnapping began."

She knitted her brows. "How's that?"

"Gary's dad said when Gary was eight they were in a used book store, and while his father was wandering in the stacks, his son found a tattered copy of *True Detective Mysteries,* a crime magazine from the 1930s, and sat down to read it."

Finger still on the trigger of her semiautomatic rifle, Virginia Winslow shrugged. "So what?"

"When Mr. Soneji found Gary, his son was sitting on the floor in the bookstore, the magazine in his lap, and staring in fascination at a picture from the Lindbergh baby's autopsy that showed the head wound in lurid detail."

She stared at me with her jaw slack, as if remembering something that frightened and appalled her.

"What is it?" I asked.

Soneji's widow hardened again. "Nothing. Doesn't surprise me. I used to catch him looking at autopsy pictures. He was always saying he was going to write a book and needed to look at them for research."

"You didn't believe him?"

"I believed him until my brother Charles noticed that Gary was always volunteering to gut deer they killed," she said. "Charles told me Gary liked to put his hands in the warm innards, said he liked the feeling, and told me how Gary'd get all bright and glowing when he was doing it."

CHAPTER 11

"I DIDN'T KNOW THAT about Gary, either," I said.

"What's this all about?" Virginia Winslow asked, studying me now.

"There was a cop shooting in DC," I said. "A man who fit Gary's description was the shooter."

I expected Soneji's widow to respond with total skepticism. But instead she looked frightened and appalled again.

"Gary's dead," she said. "*You* killed him, didn't you?"

"He killed himself," I said. "Detonated the bomb he was carrying."

Her attention flitted to the boards. "That's not what the internet is saying."

"What's the internet saying?"

"That Gary's alive," she said. "Our son, Dylan, said he's seen it online. Gary's dead, isn't he? Please tell me that."

The way she clenched the rifle told me she needed to hear it, so I said, "As far as I know, Gary Soneji's dead and has been dead for more than ten years. But someone who looked an awful lot like him shot my partner yesterday."

"What?" she said. "No."

"It's not him," I said. "I'm almost certain."

"Almost?" she said before a phone started ringing back in the house.

"I…I have to get that," she said. "Work."

"What kind of work?"

"I'm a machinist and gunsmith," she said. "My father taught me the trade."

She shut the door before I could comment. The bolts were thrown one by one.

I almost left, but then, remembering that voice I'd heard on my way in, I went around the farmhouse, seeing a small, neglected barn around which dozens of pigeons were flying.

I heard someone talking in the barn, and walked over.

Click-a-t-clack. Click-a-t-clack.

Pigeons started and whirled out the barn door.

There was a grimy window. I went to it, and peeked inside, seeing through the dirt sixteen-year-old Dylan Winslow standing there by a large pigeon coop, gazing off into space.

Dylan looked nothing like his father. He had his mother's naturally dark hair, sharp nose, and the same dull brown eyes. He was borderline obese, with hardly a chin, more a draping of his cheeks that joined a wattle above his Adam's apple.

"You need to learn your place," he said to no one. "You need to learn to be quiet. Emotional control. It's the key to a happy life."

Then he turned and walked by the pigeon coop, running a hoop of keys across the metal mesh.

Click-a-t-clack. Click-a-t-clack.

The sound rattled the pigeons and they battered themselves against their cages.

"Be quiet now," Dylan said firmly. "You got to learn some control."

Then he pivoted and started toward me, raking the cages again. *Click-a-t-clack. Click-a-t-clack.*

A disturbing little smile showed on the teen's face, and there was even more upsetting delight in his eyes. I have a PhD in criminal psychology and have studied serial killers in depth. Many of them grew up torturing animals for sport.

Had Dylan's father?

I stepped inside the barn. Gary Soneji's son had his back to me again, walking away while raking the front of the cages.

Click-a-t-clack. Click-a-t-clack.

I took another two steps and noticed a large piece of cardboard nailed to one of the barn's support posts.

There was a well-used paper target taped to the cardboard and six darts sticking out of it. The target featured a bull's-eye superimposed over a man's face. It had been used so many times that at first I didn't know who the man was.

Then I did.

"Who the hell are you?" Dylan said, and then gaped when I faced him.

"From the looks of it," I said, "I'm your dartboard."

CHAPTER 12

DYLAN WINSLOW PURSED HIS lips in long-simmering anger, said, "If Mama would let me, I'd use one of her shotguns on it instead of darts."

What do you say to the disturbed son of the disturbed criminal you shot in the face and watched burn?

"I can understand your feelings," I said.

"No, you can't," he said, sneering. "This an official visit, Detective Alex Cross?"

"As a matter of fact," I said. "A man fitting your dead father's description shot my partner in the head last night."

Dylan's sneer disappeared, replaced by widening eyes and that disturbing, delighted grin I'd seen earlier. "It's true, then, what they're saying."

"What are they saying?"

"That you didn't get my dad," Dylan said. "That he escaped the tunnels, badly wounded, but alive, and is still alive. Is that what you're telling me, too?"

There seemed so much hope in his face that, whether he was in need of psychological help or not, I didn't want to destroy it.

"If it wasn't your father who shot my partner, it was his twin."

Dylan started to laugh. He laughed so hard there were tears in his eyes.

Thumping his chest, he said, "I knew it! I felt it right here."

When he stopped, I said, "What do you think is going to happen? That he's going to suddenly appear to rescue you?"

Dylan acted as if I'd read his thoughts, but then shot back, "He will. You watch. And there's nothing you can do about it. It's like they say—Dad was always smarter than you. More patient and cunning than you."

Rather than defend myself, I said, "You're right. Your father was smarter than me, and more patient, and more cunning."

"He still is. They say so on the internet."

"What site?" I asked.

Dylan gave me that disturbing smile again before saying, "One you can't get at in a million years, Cross." He laughed. "Never in a million years."

"Really?" I said. "How about I march back up to your mother and tell her I'm coming back with a search warrant for every computer in your house?"

Dylan's grin stretched wider. "Go ahead. We don't have one."

"How about every computer in your school, in the local library, in every place your mother says you get online?"

I thought that would rock him, but it didn't.

"Knock yourself out," he said. "But unless I have a lawyer present, I am done answering your questions, and I have pigeons to feed."

Or torture, I almost said.

But I bit back the urge, and turned to leave, calling over my shoulder, "Nice to meet you, Dylan. Wonderful getting to know the son of an old enemy."

CHAPTER 13

IT WAS PAST SIX when I finally reached the ICU at GW Medical Center. The nurse at the station said Sampson's vitals had been irregular most of the day, and there'd been little if any reduction in brain swelling.

"You sick in any way?" the nurse asked.

"Not that I'm aware of. Why?"

"Protocol. The shunt draining the wound is an open track straight to the inside of your friend's healing skull. Any kind of infection could be catastrophic."

"I feel fine," I said, and put on the gown, mask, and gloves.

When I pushed open the door, Billie stirred awake in her reclining chair.

"Alex? That you?"

"The man behind the mask."

"Tell me about it," she said, getting up to hug me. "I've been wearing one the past forty hours and I'm getting rubbed raw."

"His vitals?"

Billie scanned the monitors attached to her husband and said,

"Not bad at the moment, but his blood pressure took a short, scary dive about four hours ago. I was thinking stroke until he just kind of came up out of it."

"They say talking to people in comas helps," I said.

"Stimulates the brain," she said, nodding. "But that's usually with a non-induced coma, when there aren't drugs involved."

"All the same," I said, and went to Sampson's side.

"I'll be a few minutes," Billie said.

"Be right here until you get back," I said.

When she'd gone out, I held Sampson's giant hand and gave him an account of the day's investigation, sparing him no detail. It felt good and familiar, and right, to talk it out with him, as if Sampson were not drugged down to the reptilian part of his brain, but acute and thoughtful and funny as hell.

"That's it," I said. "And, yes, I want another crack at Soneji's widow and kid before long."

The door opened. Billie stepped back inside, and then several of the monitors around Sampson began to squawk in alarm.

A team burst in. I was pushed to the corner with Billie.

"It's his blood pressure again," Billie said in a wavering voice. "Jesus, I don't know if his heart can take this much longer."

Ninety seconds later, the crisis passed and his vitals improved.

"I don't know what happened," I said, bewildered. "I was telling him about the investigation and…"

"What?" Billie said. "Why did you do that?"

"Because he'd want to know."

"No," she said, shaking her head. "That's done. That's over, Alex."

"What's over?"

"His career as a cop," Billie said. "No matter how he recovers, that part of John's life is over if he wants to continue to be my husband."

"John loves being a cop," I said.

"I know he does…did…but that's over," Billie said sharply. "I will care for him, and defend John until the day one of us dies, but between now and then, his days carrying a gun and a badge are behind him."

CHAPTER 14

"SHE'S GOT THE RIGHT to demand that," Bree said later in the hospital cafeteria. "John took a bullet to the head, Alex."

"I know," I said, frustrated and heartsick.

It felt like part of John had died and was never coming back. And it would never be the same between us, as partners anyway. That was dead, too.

I explained this to Bree, and she put her hands on mine and said, "You'll never have a better friend than John Sampson. That friendship, that fierce bond you two have, will never be broken, even if he's no longer a cop, even if he's no longer your partner. Okay?"

"No," I said, pushing my plate away. "But I'll have to learn to live with it."

"You haven't eaten three bites," Bree said, gesturing at the plate.

"No appetite," I said.

"Then force yourself," Bree said. "Especially the protein. Your brain has to be tip-top if you're going to find Soneji."

I laughed softly. "You're always looking out for me."

"Every moment I can, baby."

I ate quite a bit more, and washed it down with three full glasses of water.

"Not quite Nana Mama's cooking," I said.

"I'm sure there'll be leftovers," Bree said.

"You trying to get me fat?" I said.

"I like a little cushion."

I didn't know what to say to that, and we both burst out laughing. Then I looked over and saw Billie standing in the doorway, watching us with bitterness and longing in her expression. She turned and left.

"Should I go after her?" I asked.

"No," Bree said. "I'll talk to her tomorrow."

"Home?"

"Home."

We left the hospital and were crossing a triangular plaza to the Foggy Bottom Metro station when the first shot rang out.

I heard the flat crack of the muzzle blast. I felt the bullet rip past my left ear, grabbed Bree, and yanked her to the ground by two newspaper boxes. People were screaming and scattering.

"Where is he?" Bree said.

"I don't know," I said, before the second and third shots shattered the glass of one newspaper rack and *ping*ed off another.

Then I heard squealing tires, and jumped up in time to see a white panel van roar north on 23rd Street, Northwest, heading toward Washington Circle, and a dozen different escape routes. As the van flashed past us, I caught a glimpse of the driver.

Gary Soneji was looking my way as if posing for a mental picture, grinning like a lunatic and holding his right-hand thumb up, index finger extended, like a gun he was aiming right at me.

I was so shocked that another instant passed before I started running across the plaza to 23rd, trying to get a look at his license plates. But his plate lights were dark, and the van soon disappeared into evening traffic, headed in the direction of whatever hellhole Gary Soneji was calling home these days.

"Did you see him?" I asked Bree, who was shaken, but calling in the shots to dispatch.

She shook her head after she'd finished. "You did?"

"It was him, Bree. Gary Soneji in the flesh. As if he hadn't been blown up and burned, as if he hadn't spent the past decade in a box under six feet of dirt."

CHAPTER 15

THE NEXT MORNING, I called GW to check on Sampson. His vitals had destabilized again.

Part of me said, *Go to the hospital,* but instead I drove out to Quantico, Virginia, and the FBI Lab.

For almost seven years, I worked for the Bureau in the behavioral science department as a full-time consultant and left on good terms. I have many friends who still work at Quantico, including my old partner, Ned Mahoney.

I called ahead, and he met me at the gate, made sure I got the VIP treatment clearing security.

"What are friends in high places for?" Mahoney asked when I thanked him. "How's John?"

I gave him a brief update on Sampson and my investigation.

"How could Soneji be alive?" Mahoney said. "I was there, remember? I saw him burning, too. It was him. "

"Then who was the guy who shot Sampson and tried to shoot me last night?" I said. "Because both times I've seen him, my brain has screamed *Soneji!* Both times."

"Hey, hey, Alex," Mahoney said, patting me on the shoulder out of concern. "Take a big breath. If it's him, we'll help you find him."

I took several deep, long breaths, trying to keep my thoughts from whirling, and said, "Let's start with the cybercrime unit."

Ten minutes later, we went through an unmarked door into a large space filled with low-walled cubicles that were in a soft blue light Mahoney said was supposed to increase productivity. There were three, sometimes four computer screens at every workstation.

"The only thing that separates the IT brainpower in this room from a company like Google is the dress code," Mahoney said.

"No Ping-Pong, either," I said.

"There's agitation in that direction," Mahoney said, weaving through the cubicles.

"Any chance it happens?"

"When the Bureau starts admitting J. Edgar preferred panties," he said, and then stopped in front of a workstation in the middle of the room.

"Agent Batra?" Mahoney said. "I want to introduce you to Alex Cross."

A petite Indian woman in her late twenties in a conservative blue suit and black pumps spun around from one of four screens at her station. She stood quickly and put out her hand, so small it felt like a doll's.

"Special Agent Henna Batra," she said. "An honor to meet you, Dr. Cross."

"And you as well."

"Agent Batra is said to be at one with the internet," Mahoney said. "If anyone can help you, she can. Stop by the office on your way out, Alex."

"Will do," I said.

"So," Agent Batra said, sitting again. "What are you looking for?"

"A website where there are active conversations going on concerning Gary Soneji."

"I know that case," Batra said. "We studied it at the academy. He's dead."

"Evidently his admirers don't think so, and I'd like to see what they're saying about Soneji. I was warned we'd never find the site in a million years."

With Special Agent Batra navigating the web via a link to a supercomputer, the search took all of fourteen minutes.

"Quite a few that mention Soneji," Batra said, gesturing at the screen, and then scrolling down before tapping on a link. "But I'm betting this is the one you're looking for."

I squinted to read the link. "ZRXQT?"

"Anonymous, or at least attempting anonymity," Batra said. "And it's locked and encrypted. But I ran a filter that picked up traces of commands going into and out of that website. The density of Soneji mentions in those traces is through the roof compared to every other site that talks about him."

"You can't get in?"

"I didn't say that," Batra said, as if I'd insulted her. "You drink tea?"

"Coffee," I said.

She gestured across the room. "There's a break room over there. If you'd be so kind as to bring me some hot tea, Dr. Cross. I should be able to get inside by the time you come back."

I thought it was kind of funny that Batra had started the conversation as my subordinate and was now ordering me around. Then again, I hadn't a clue about how she was doing what she was doing. Then again, she was at one with the internet.

"Oolong?" I asked.

"Fine," Batra said, already engrossed in her work.

I found the coffee and the tea, but when I returned, she was still typing.

"Got it?"

"Not yet," she said, irritated. "It's sophisticated, multilevel, and…"

Lines of code began to fill the page. Batra seemed to speed-read the code as it rolled by, because, after twenty seconds of this, she said, "Oh, of course."

She gave the computer another command, and a homepage appeared, featuring a cement wall in some abandoned building. Across the wall in dripping black graffiti letters, it read *Long Live The Soneji!*

CHAPTER 16

I WON'T BORE YOU with a page-by-page description of the www
.thesoneji.net website. There may be archives of it still up on the
internet for those interested.

For those of you less inclined to explore the dark side of the
web, it's enough to know that Gary Soneji had developed a cult
of personality in the decade since I'd seen him burn, hundreds of
digital devotees who worshipped him with the kind of fervor I'd
previously assigned to Appalachian snake handlers and the Hare
Krishnas.

They called themselves The Soneji, and they seemed to know
almost every nuance of the life of the kidnapper and mass mur-
derer. In addition to an extensive biography, there were hundreds
of lurid photos, links to articles, and an online chat forum where
members hotly debated all things Soneji.

The hottest topics?

Number one that day was *the John Sampson shooting*.

The Soneji were generally ecstatic that my partner had been
shot and barely clung to life, but a few posts stood out.

Napper2 wrote, Gary fuckin' got Sampson!

Gary's so back, The Waste Man agreed.

Only thing better would be Cross on a Cross, wrote Black Hole.

That day's coming sooner than later, said Gary's Girl. Gary's missed Cross twice. He won't miss a third time.

Aside from being the subject of homicidal speculation, something bothered me about that last post, the one from Gary's Girl. I studied it and the others, trying to figure out what was different.

"They think he's alive," Agent Batra offered.

"Yeah, that's hot thread number two," I said. "Let's take a look there, and come back."

She clicked on the "Resurrection Man" thread.

Cross saw him, came face to face with Gary, wrote Sapper9. Shit his pants, is what I heard.

Cross was hit in first attack, wrote Chosen One. Soneji's aim is true. Cross is just lucky.

Beemer answered, My respect for Gary is profound, but he is not alive. That is impossible.

The believers among The Soneji went berserk on Beemer for having the gall to challenge the consensus. Beemer was attacked from all sides. To his credit, Beemer fought back.

Call me Doubting Thomas, but show me the evidence. Can I put my finger through Soneji's hand? Can I see where the lance pierced his side?

You could if he trusted you the way he trusts me, wrote Gary's Girl.

Beemer wrote, So you've seen him, GG?

After a long pause, Gary's Girl wrote, I have. With my own two eyes.

Pic? Beemer said.

A minute passed, and then two. Five minutes after his demand, Beemer wrote, Funny how illusions can seem so real.

A second later the screen blinked and a picture appeared.

Taken at night, it was a selfie of a big, muscular woman gone goth, heavy on the black on black right down to the lipstick. She was grinning raunchily and sitting in the lap of a man with wispy red hair. His hands held her across her deep, leather-clad cleavage, and he had buried three quarters of his face into the side of her neck.

The other quarter, however, including his right eye, was clearly visible.

He was staring right into the camera with an amused and lecherous expression that seemed designed to taunt the lens and me. He knew I'd see the picture someday and be infuriated.

I was sure of that. It was the kind of thing Soneji would do.

"That him?" Batra asked. "Gary Soneji?"

"Close enough. Can you track down Gary's Girl?"

The FBI cyber agent thought about that, and then said, "Give me twenty minutes, maybe less."

CHAPTER 17

AT FIVE O'CLOCK THAT afternoon, Bree and I drove through the tiny rural community of Flintstone, Maryland, past the Flintstone Post Office, the Stone Age Café, and Carl's Gas and Grub.

We found a side street off Route 144, and drove down a wooded lane to a freshly painted green ranch house set off all by itself in a meticulously tended yard. A shiny new Audi Q5 sat in the driveway.

"I thought you said she's on welfare," Bree said.

"Food stamps, too," I said.

We parked behind the Audi and got out. AC/DC was blasting from inside the house. We went to the front door and found it ajar.

I tried the bell. It was broken.

Bree knocked and called out, "Delilah Pinder?"

We heard nothing in response but the howling of an electric guitar against a thundering baseline.

"Door's open," I said. "We're checking on her well-being."

"Be my guest," Bree said.

I pushed open the door and found myself in a room decorated

with brand-new leather furniture and a big curved HD television. The music throbbed on from somewhere deeper inside the house.

We checked the kitchen, saw boxes of appliances that hadn't even been opened, and then headed down the hallway toward the source of the music. The first door on the left was a home gym with Olympic weight-lifting equipment. The music came from the room at the end of the hall.

There was a lull in the song, just enough that I heard a woman's voice cry, "That's it!" before the throbbing, wailing song drowned her out.

The door to that room at the end of the hall was cracked open two inches. A brilliant light shone through.

"Delilah Pinder?" I called out.

No answer.

I stepped forward and pushed the door open enough to get a comprehensive view of a very muscular and artificially busty woman up on all fours on a four-poster bed. Gyrating her hips in time with the beat, she was naked, and looking over her shoulder at a GoPro camera mounted on a tripod.

I just stood there, stunned for a moment, long enough for Bree to nudge me, and long enough for Delilah Pinder to look around and spot me.

"Christ!" she screamed and flung herself forward on the bed.

I thought she was diving for modesty, but she hit some kind of panic button and the door slammed shut in my face and locked.

"What the hell just happened?" Bree demanded.

"I think she was doing a live sex show on the internet," I said.

"No."

"I swear," I said.

The music shut off and a woman shouted, "Goddamnit, whoever you are, I'm calling the sheriff. They are going to hunt you down!"

"We are the police, Miss Pinder," Bree yelled back.

"What the hell are you doing in my house, then?" she screamed. "I've got rights, and you had no right to come into my house or place of business!"

"You're correct," I said. "But we knocked and called out, and we felt we were doing a safety check on you."

"What I do here is perfectly legal," she said. "So please leave."

"We aren't here about your, uh, business," Bree said.

"Who are you, then? What do you want?"

"My name is Alex Cross. I'm a detective with the DC Metro Police, and I'm here concerning Gary's Girl."

There was a long silence, and then the music cranked up. But over it I heard the sound of a door slamming loudly.

"She's running," Bree said, spun around, and took off.

CHAPTER 18

I CAN HOLD MY own in the weight room, but I am no match for Bree in a footrace. She exploded back through the house and barreled out the front door.

Delilah Pinder, who was now dressed in a blue warm-up suit and running shoes, had already sprinted around the end of the house and was charging across the front lawn, heading for the road. I came out the front door in time to see Bree try to tackle the big woman.

Delilah saw her coming and stuck out her hand like a seasoned running back, hitting Bree in the chest. Bree stumbled. The internet sex star raced out onto the road and headed toward the highway.

I cut diagonally through the yard, trying to close in on her from the side. But when I broke through the trees and jumped the stone wall onto the road, Bree was right back behind Pinder.

She jumped on the much bigger woman's back, threw an arm bar around her neck, and choked her. Delilah tried to buck her off, and to pry her hold apart. But Bree held on tight.

Finally, the big woman stopped running. Her massive thighs wobbled, and she sat down hard at Bree's feet.

"Oh, my God," Bree gasped when I ran up. "That was like 'Meet the Amazon.'"

"More like 'Ride the Amazon,'" I said, as she put zip ties on Delilah's wrists.

The woman was regaining her strength. She struggled against the restraints.

"No," she said. "Let me go."

"Not for a while yet," I said, picking her up.

Delilah twisted her head around in a rage, and spit in my face.

"Knock that off!" Bree shouted, and wrenched up hard on Delilah's bound wrists. "That kind of bullshit gets you in trouble, and you're already in a world of trouble. Got it?"

Delilah was obviously in pain, and finally nodded.

Bree eased up on the pressure while I used a tissue to wipe my face.

"I don't know what this is about," Delilah said. "I told you, I have a legitimate business, registered with the state and everything. Delilah Entertainment. Check it out."

"You know exactly what this is about," I said, grabbing one of her formidable biceps and marching her back toward her house. "You're a member of The Soneji. You're Gary's Girl. You like to take selfies of you and Gary together. Isn't that true?"

Delilah looked at me smugly and said, "Every single word of it, Cross. Every single word."

"Where is Gary Soneji?" Bree asked.

"I have no idea," Delilah said. "Gary comes and goes as he pleases. Our relationship is strong enough for that."

"Yeah, I'm sure it is," I said, rolling my eyes. "But you understand you've abetted a man who shot a police officer in cold blood?"

"How's that?"

"You housed him," Bree said. "You fed him. You dressed up goth and had sex with him, maybe even did one of your kinky shows for him."

"Every night, darling," Delilah said. "He loved it. So did I. And that's where yours truly will shut up. I have the right to remain silent. And I have a right to an attorney. I'm taking both those rights, right here and right now."

CHAPTER 19

PALE MORNING FOG SHROUDED much of the cemetery from my view. The fog swirled on the wet grass, the melting snow that remained, and the gravestones. It left droplets on the pile of wilted flower bouquets and empty liquor bottles and remembrances that had to be moved before the backhoe could begin its work.

The last item was a baby doll, naked, with lipstick smeared on the lips.

Shivering against the dank March air, I zipped my police slicker higher and pulled on the hood. I stood off to one side of the grave with Bill Worden, the cemetery superintendent, alternately looking at the baby doll and watching the backhoe claw deeper into the soil. A baby doll, I thought, recalling a real baby tossed through the air with total indifference, if not cruelty.

Someone brought that doll here, I thought. In celebration. In reverence.

That's just sick. How could you worship that?

I glanced at the headstone Worden dug from the ground after I'd brought him an order from a federal judge in Trenton.

The grave marker was simple. Rectangular black polished granite.

"G. Soneji" was etched in the face, along with the date of his birth. The date of his death, however, had been chiseled away. That was it. No mention of his brutal crimes or his disturbing life.

The man six feet under the headstone was all but anonymous.

And yet they'd come. The Soneji. They'd chipped away at the gravestone. Spray-painted the grass to read *"Soneji Lives."* I took pictures before the backhoe destroyed it.

"How many visit?" I asked over the sound of the digging machine.

Worden, the cemetery superintendent, tugged his hood over his head and said, "Hard to say. It's not like we keep it under surveillance. But a fair number every month."

"Enough to leave that pile of flowers," I said, eyeing the baby doll again.

Worden nodded. "For some it seems almost like a pilgrimage."

"Yeah, except Mr. Soneji was no saint," I said.

Drizzle began to fall, forcing me deeper into the collar of my jacket. A few moments later, the backhoe turned off.

"There's the straps, Bill," the equipment operator said. "I'll hand-dig the last of it."

"No need," Worden said. "Just hook up and lift, brush the dirt off later."

The backhoe operator shrugged and got out cables, which he attached to the bucket. Then he got down into the grave and clipped the cables to the rings of stout straps that had been left after the casket was lowered.

"They're not weakened by being in the dirt ten years?" I asked.

Worden shook his head. "Not unless something chewed through them."

The superintendent was right. When the backhoe arm rose, the straps easily lifted the casket of a man I helped kill.

Wet dirt slid and cascaded off the top of the casket as it came free of the grave and dangled four feet above the hole. The wind picked up. The casket swayed.

"Put it down there," Worden said, gesturing to one side.

I was fixated on the casket, wondering what was inside, beyond the charred remains I'd seen placed in a body bag beneath Grand Central Station a decade before. He was in there, wasn't he?

Every instinct said yes. But…

As the casket swung and lowered, I happened to look beyond it and between two far monuments. The wind had blown a narrow vent in the fog. I could see a slice of the graveyard between those monuments that ran all the way to the pine barrens that surrounded the cemetery.

Standing at the edge of the woods, perhaps eighty yards from me, was a man in a green rain slicker. He was turning away. When his back was to me, he pulled off his hood, revealing a head of thinning red hair. Then he raised his right hand, and pointed his middle finger at the sky.

And me.

CHAPTER 20

I STOOD THERE, TOO stunned to move for the moment it took for the wind to ebb and the fog to creep back, obscuring the figure, who stepped into the pine barrens and disappeared.

Then my shock evaporated, and I took off, drawing my pistol as I sprinted between the gravestones. Peering through the fog gathering again in the cemetery, I tried to figure out exactly where I'd seen him go into the pines.

There it was, those two monuments. He'd been framed between them. I ran to the spot and looked back toward the fog-obscured backhoe and the exhumed casket. When I thought I had the correct bearings, I turned and headed in a straight line toward the edge of the forest.

"Dr. Cross?" the superintendent called after me. "Where are you going?"

I ignored him and charged to the edge of the dripping pines, scanning the ground and seeing a scuff mark that looked fresh, not yet beaten down by the rain. I pushed my way into the trees.

The forest was thick there, crowded with young saplings with wet branches that bent away and wet needles that slid past my clothes. I stopped, unsure where to go, but then noticed a broken branch on the ground.

The inner wood looked bright and new. So did the broken branch to my left at ten o'clock. I went that way for fifty, maybe seventy-five yards, and then broke into an expanse of older trees, more than ten feet high, and growing in long straight rows, a pine plantation.

Despite the fog, I soon spotted dark, discolored spots on the mat of dead needles that covered the forest floor. I went to them, and saw where he'd kicked up the duff as he'd run down one of those lanes through the trees.

I ran after him, wondering if I could catch up, and numerous times whether I'd lost the way. But then I'd find some disturbance in the pine needles and push on one hundred, two hundred, three hundred yards deeper into the barrens.

What direction was I going? I had no idea, and it didn't matter. As long as Soneji was leaving signs, I was staying with him. I thought I'd cross a logging road or trail at some point, but didn't. There was just the monotony of the plantation pines and the swirling fog.

Then the way began to climb up a hill. I could clearly see where he'd had to dig in the edges of his shoes to keep his footing, and more broken branches.

When I hit the top of the knoll, there was a clearing of sorts with a jumble of tree trunks to one side, as if a windstorm had blown them over. I skirted the jumble, crossed the hilltop, and found myself looking down into a long, broad valley of mature pines.

The forest had been thinned there, as if some of the trees had already been harvested. Despite the fog, I could see down a dozen lanes and deeper into the woods than at any other time since I'd entered it. Nothing moved below me.

Nothing at—

A rifle cracked. The bark of a tree next to me exploded and I dove for the ground behind one of those downed tree trunks.

Where was he?

The shot came from the valley. I was sure of it. But where down there?

"Cross?" he called. "I'm coming for you, even from the grave if I have to."

If it wasn't him, he'd studied Soneji's voice, right down to the inflection.

When I didn't answer, he shouted, "Hear me, Cross?"

He sounded to my right and below me, no more than seventy yards. Raising my head as high as I dared, I scanned the valley there. The fog was in and out, but I thought I'd see him move or adjust his angle if he wanted another shot at me.

But I couldn't make him out.

"I know I didn't hit you," he called, his voice cracking weirdly. "I did, you would have gone down like the shit bag you are."

I decided not to engage, to let him think he'd gotten lucky, taken me out with one bullet. And it was odd the way his voice had cracked, wasn't it? Gone to a higher pitch?"

Tense moments passed, a minute and then two, while my eyes darted back and forth, trying to spot him, hoping he'd come in to make sure of the kill.

"How's your partner?" he called, and I heard him chuckle hoarsely. "He took a hit, didn't he? What I hear, best-case scenario, he'll be a veg."

It took every fiber of my being, but I did not engage with him, even then. I just lay there and waited, scanning and scanning and scanning.

I never saw him go, or heard anything like a distant twig breaking to suggest he was on the move again. He never said another word, and nothing told me he'd left but the time that kept ticking away.

I lowered my head after ten minutes and dug out my phone. No service.

The rain started in earnest then, drumming, beating down the fog and revealing the plantation. Nothing moved but a doe a hundred yards out.

I wanted to get up and go down there, look for him. But if he was waiting, I'd be exposed again. After fifteen more minutes of watching, I crawled back in the direction I'd come until I was well down the backside of the hill.

There was a bitter taste in my mouth when I got to my feet and started back toward the cemetery.

I hadn't gotten halfway there when my cell phone buzzed in my pocket.

A text from Billie.

"Alex, wherever you are, come. John's taken a bad turn. We're on deathwatch here."

CHAPTER 21

BY THE TIME I reached the cemetery, the superintendent had already loaded the casket into the FBI van that would take it to Quantico for examination. I explained the urgency of my situation, and left.

I called ahead to New Jersey, Delaware, and Maryland state police dispatchers, asking for help. When I reached I-95, there were two Jersey state trooper cruisers waiting. One in front, the other behind, they escorted me to the border, where two Delaware cruisers met me. Two more waited when I reached the Maryland line. At times we were going more than a hundred.

Less than two hours after I'd read the text, I got off the elevator to the ICU at GW Medical Center, still in damp clothes and chilled as I ran down the all-too-familiar halls to the waiting area. Billie sat at the back, her feet drawn up under her. Her elbows rested across her knees and she had a skeptical, faraway look in her eye, as if she couldn't believe that God was doing this to her.

Bree sat at her left, Nana Mama on her right.

"What happened?" I asked.

"They decided to bring him up out of the chemical coma," Billie said, tears streaming down her cheeks.

"He flatlined. They had to paddle him," Bree said. "He came back, but his vitals are turning against him."

"Billie's called in the priest," Nana Mama said. "He's giving John the last rites."

Whatever control I'd maintained until that point evaporated and I began to grieve in gasps of disbelief and an explosion of sorrow and tears. It was real. My best friend, the indestructible one, Big John Sampson, was going to die.

I sank into a chair and sobbed. Bree came over and hugged me. I leaned into her and cried some more.

The priest came in. "He's in God's hands now," he said, consoling us. "The doctor says there's nothing more they can do for him."

"Can we go in?" Billie asked.

"Of course," he said.

Nana Mama, Billie, and Bree got up. I looked at them, feeling numb.

"I can't do it," I said, feeling helpless. "I just can't watch this. Can you forgive me?"

"I don't want to either, Alex," Billie said. "But I want him to hear my voice one last time before he goes."

Nana Mama patted me on the shoulders as she followed Billie into the ICU. Bree asked if I wanted her to stay, and I shook my head.

"Going in there scares me more than anything has in my entire life," I said. "I need to take a walk, get my courage up."

"And pray," she said, kissed me on the head, and went inside.

I got up and felt like a coward walking toward the men's room. I went inside and washed my face, trying to think of anything but John and all the good times we'd had over the years, playing football and basketball, attending the police academy, and finding our way through the ranks to detective and partners against crime.

That would never happen again. John and me would never happen again.

I left the restroom and wandered off through the medical complex, sure that any minute now I'd get a text that he was gone. Guilt built up in me at the thought that after all we'd been through, I wouldn't be there at Sampson's side when he passed.

I stopped and almost turned around. Then noticed I was standing outside the plastic surgery offices. A beautiful Ethiopian-looking woman in a white jacket came out the door.

She smiled at me. Her teeth gleamed and her facial skin was so taut and smooth she could have been thirty. Then again, she could have been sixty and often under the knife.

"Dr. Coleman?" I said, reading her badge.

She stopped and said, "Yes?"

I showed her my badge, said, "I could use your help."

"Yes?" she said, looking worried. "How so?"

"I'm investigating the shooting of a police officer," I said. "We want to know, how difficult would it be to make one person look almost exactly like another?"

She squinted. "You mean, good enough to be an imposter?"

"Yes," I said. "Is it possible?"

"That depends," Dr. Coleman said, glancing at her watch. "Can you walk with me? I have to give a lecture about twenty minutes from here."

"Yes," I said, glad for the diversion.

We walked through the medical center and out the other side, ending up on the George Washington University campus. Along the way, the plastic surgeon said that similar facial structure would be key to surgically altering a person to look like someone else.

"The closer the subject was to looking like the original to begin with, the better the results," she said. "After that it would all be in the skill of the surgeon."

"So, even the similar bone structure wouldn't guarantee success for your everyday surgeon?"

Dr. Coleman smiled. "If the end product is as close to the original as you say it is, then there is no way an average boob-job surgeon did it. You're looking for a scalpel artist, Detective."

"What kind of money are we talking?"

"Depends on the extent of surgical alteration required," she said. "But I'm thinking this is a hundred-thousand-dollar job, maybe less in Brazil."

A hundred thousand dollars? Who would spend that much to look like Gary Soneji? Or go to Brazil to get it done?

I felt my phone buzz in my pocket, and sickened.

"Here I am," Dr. Coleman said, stopping outside one of the university's many buildings. "Any more questions, Detective?"

"No," I said, handing her a card. "But if I do, can I call?"

"Absolutely," she said, and hurried inside.

I swallowed hard and then got out my phone.

The text was from Bree: "Come now or you'll regret it the rest of your life."

I started to run.

Ten minutes later, I went through the door of the ICU, trying to keep my emotions from ruining me all over again.

When I reached the doorway to John's room, Billie, Bree, and Nana Mama were all sobbing.

I thought I'd come too late, that I'd done my best friend and brother the ultimate disservice, and not been there when he took his last breath.

Then I realized they were all sobbing for joy.

"It's a miracle, Alex," Bree said, tears streaming down her cheeks. "Look."

I stepped inside the crowded room. A nurse and a doctor were working feverishly on John. He was still on his back in bed, still on the ventilator, still hitched up to a dozen different monitors.

But his eyes were open and roving lazily.

CHAPTER 22

WE SAT WITH JOHN for hours as more of the drugs wore off. They removed his breathing tube, and he came more and more to consciousness.

John did not acknowledge his name when Billie called it softly, trying to get him to turn his head to her. At first Sampson seemed not even to know where he was, as if he were lost in some dream.

But then, after the first nap, he did hear his wife, and his face lolled toward her. Then he moved his fingers and toes on command, and lifted both arms.

When I sat beside him and held his hand, his lips kept opening as if he wanted to talk. No sound came out, and he appeared frustrated.

"It's okay, buddy," I said, holding tight. "We know you love us."

Sampson relaxed and slept again. When he awoke, Elizabeth Navilus, a top speech-language pathologist, was waiting. She was part of a team of specialists rotating through the room, performing the various exams on the JFK Coma Recovery Scale, a method of diagnosing the extent of brain damage.

Navilus ran Sampson through a brief battery of tests. She found that John's cognitive awareness as expressed through his language comprehension was growing by the moment. But he was having trouble speaking. The best he could do was chew at the air and hum.

It crushed me.

Out in the waiting area, Navilus told us to take hope from the fact that head trauma patients often exhibit understanding before being able to respond.

Later, when Nana Mama had left for home to cook dinner, and Bree to the office, and Billie to the cafeteria, I sat by John's side.

"I was there when you were shot," I told him. "It was Soneji. Or someone who looked just like him."

Sampson blinked, and then nodded.

"I came close to catching him this morning," I said. "He was watching when we dug up Soneji's body."

He looked away and closed his eyes.

"I'm going to get him, John," I said. "I promise you."

He barely nodded before sagging off to sleep.

Sitting there, watching him, I felt better, stronger, and more humbled and in debt to my Lord and savior than ever before. The idea of Sampson dying must have been as much of an abomination to God as I thought it was.

If that wasn't a miracle, I don't know what is.

CHAPTER 23

I STAYED AT THE hospital until nine, promised Billie I'd be back in the morning, and headed home. Given what had happened the last time I'd exited GW Medical Center and looked for a cab, my head was turning three-sixty.

I saw no threat, however, and stepped to the curb. As I did, Soneji's voice from earlier in the day echoed back to me.

I'm coming for you, even from the grave if I have to.

It sounded so much like Gary, it was scary. I'd had multiple conversations with him over the years, and Soneji's tone and delivery were unmistakable.

After I'd gotten into the cab and given the driver my home address, I almost pushed these thoughts aside. But then I blinked, remembering how his voice had cracked weirdly and turned hoarse when he said, "I know I didn't hit you. I did, you would have gone down like the shit bag you are."

It sounded like he had something wrong in his throat. Cancer? Polyps? Or were his vocal cords just straining under the tensions wound up inside him?

I tried to remember every nuance of our encounter in the pine barrens, the way he'd swaggered into the trees, finger held high. Where was the gun then? Had he been trying to lure me in for a shot?

In retrospect, it felt like he had, and I'd fallen for it. Where was all the training I'd done? The protocol? I'd reacted on emotion, charging into the pines after him. Just the way Soneji had wanted me to.

That bothered me because it made me realize that Soneji understood me, could predict my impulses the way I could predict his a dozen years before. I mean, how else would he have known to be at the cemetery when I was there to exhume his body? What or who had tipped him?

I had no answers for that other than the possibility Soneji or The Soneji had us bugged. Or had it just seemed the rational thing to do at some point, given the fact that I'd seen someone who looked just like him at least three times now?

These unanswerable questions weighed on me the entire ride home. I felt depressed climbing from the taxi and waiting for the receipt. Soneji, or whoever, was thinking ahead of me, plotting, hatching, and acting before I could respond.

Climbing the porch stairs, I was beginning to feel like I was a fish on a hook with some angler toying with me, messing with my lip.

But the second I stepped inside the house, smelled something savory coming from Nana Mama's kitchen, and heard my son, Ali, laughing, I let it go. I let everything about the sonofabitch go.

"Dad?" Jannie said, coming down the stairs. "How's John?"

"He's got a fight and a half ahead of him, but he's alive."

"Nana Mama said it's, like, a miracle."

"I'd have to agree," I said, and hugged her tight.

"Dad, look at this," Ali called. "You can't believe how good this looks."

"The new TV," Jannie said. "It's pretty amazing."

"What new TV?"

"Nana Mama and Ali ordered it off the internet. They just installed it."

I stepped into our once cozy television room to see it had been transformed into a home theater, with new leather chairs, and a huge, curved 4K resolution HD screen on the far wall. Ali had on a repeat of *The Walking Dead,* one of his favorites, and the zombies looked like they were right there in the room with us.

"You should see when we switch it to 3D, Dad!" Ali said. "It's crazy!"

"I can see that," I said. "Does it do basketball?"

Ali took his eyes off the screen. "They're right in the room with you."

I smiled. "You'll have to show me after dinner."

"I can do that," Ali said. "Show you how to run it from your laptop."

I gave him the thumbs up, and then wandered through the dining room to the kitchen upgrade and great room addition we'd put on two years before.

Nana Mama was bustling at her command-center stove.

"Roast chicken, sweet potato fries, broccoli with almonds, and a nice salad," she said. "How's John?"

"Sleeping when I left," I said. "And dinner sounds great. Nice TV."

She made a deep inhaling sound, and said, "Isn't it? I can't wait to see *Masterpiece Theatre* on there. That *Downton Abbey* show."

"I was thinking the same thing," I said.

Nana Mama looked over her shoulder, gave me a sour, threatening look, and said, "Don't you be mocking me, now."

"I wouldn't dream of it, Nana," I said, trying to hide the smile that wanted to creep onto my face. "Oh, I thought you said you weren't going to let the lottery money change our lives."

"I said I didn't want some big mansion to get lost in," she snapped. "Or tooling around in some ridiculous car. But that doesn't mean we can't have some nice things in this house, and still do some good for people. Which reminds me, when is my hot-breakfast program going to be able to start up again?"

I held up my hands. "I'll find out tonight."

"I'm not getting any younger, and I want to see that ongoing," she said. "Endowed. And that reading program for kids."

"Yes, ma'am, and you're sure you're not getting younger? Isn't there a painting of you in some attic that shows your real age?"

She tried to fight it, but that brought on a smile. "Aren't you just the smoothest talker in—?"

"Dad?" Ali cried, running into the kitchen.

He looked petrified, on the verge of crying.

"What's the matter?"

"Someone's taken over my computer," he said.

"What?" Nana Mama said.

"There's this crazy man on the screen now, not *The Walking Dead,* and he won't turn off. He's holding a baby and saying, like, over and over that he's going to come for you, Dad, even from the grave."

CHAPTER 24

IN THE VIDEO CLIP, Gary Soneji was just as I remembered him: out on one of Grand Central Station's train platforms, holding the infant, and taunting me.

I'd never seen the video. Never knew it existed, but it was definitely legitimate. After viewing the clip six or seven times, I could see my own shadow stretched in the space between me and Gary Soneji. The camera operator all those years ago had to have been right off my left shoulder.

Was the cameraman a fluke? A random passerby? Or someone working with Soneji?

The clip started again. It appeared on endless loop.

"Dad, this is giving me the creeps," Jannie said. "Turn it off."

"Gimme the remote and the computer, Ali," I said.

"I've got homework on this computer," he said.

"I'll transfer your homework to the one in the kitchen," I said, and gave him a gimme motion.

He groaned and handed it to me.

Bree came in the front door. I hit the Power button on the remote, but the screen did not turn off. Instead, it broke from that endless loop to Kelly green.

I tried to turn the screen off again, but it jumped to black, slashed diagonally with a golden beam of light. The camera zoomed closer to that light and you could see a silhouette of a person there.

Closer, it was a man.

Closer still, and it was Soneji.

He was giving the lens the same quarter profile we'd seen in the still image that Gary's Girl posted on the website forum, the one where his eye and the corner of his mouth conspired to leer right at me.

But this time Soneji spoke.

In that cracking, hoarse voice I'd heard earlier that day in the pine barrens, Soneji said, "You're not safe in the trees, Cross. You're not safe in your own home. The Soneji are everywhere!"

Then he threw his head back, and barked and brayed his laughter before the screen froze. A title appeared below: www .thesoneji.net.

"What's that, Dad?" Ali asked, upset.

I stormed to the screen, followed the cord to its power source, and tore it violently out of the wall.

"Alex?" Bree said. "What's going on?"

I looked at Ali. "Was that *Walking Dead* episode streaming from Netflix?"

"Yes."

Yanking out my cell phone, I looked to Bree and said, "Soneji hacked into our internet feed."

"I'll shut the router down," Bree said.

"No, don't," I said. I scrolled through my recent calls and hit Call. "I have a feeling it will be better if the link's still active."

The phone picked up. "Yes?"

"This is Alex Cross," I said. "How fast can you get to my house?"

Forty minutes later, as we were finishing up Nana Mama's roast chicken masterpiece, and fighting over who was going to get the last wing and who the last sweet potato fries, there was a sharp knock at our side door.

"I'll get it," I said, put my napkin down, and went out into the great room and unlocked the door that led to the side yard and the alley behind our place.

I did not turn on the light, just opened it quickly and let our visitors inside. The first was Ned Mahoney, my former partner at the FBI. The second was Special Agent Henna Batra of the Bureau's cybercrime unit.

"Who's making sure you're safe in your own home?" Mahoney asked once I'd closed the door.

"Metro in unmarked cars, both ends of the block," I said.

"Soneji's still the type to try."

"I know," I said. "But I think we're good."

"I'm still unclear why you wanted me here, Dr. Cross," Agent Batra said.

"I think Soneji or The Soneji may have made a mistake," I said. "If I'm right, they left a digital trail inside my house, or on our network, anyway."

CHAPTER 25

I GOT TO GW Medical Center early the following morning with my children's howls ringing in my head. Special Agent Batra had taken every computer and phone in the house to Quantico. She'd promised to work as fast as she could, but it was like they'd lost their right hands when the phones were taken away.

I kind of felt the same way walking to Sampson's room, and decided to buy a cheap phone afterward. I was happy to find John sitting up and drinking through a straw.

Billie hadn't arrived yet, so I'd gotten to sit with him awhile, and brought him up to date on all that had occurred the prior day. Though his eyes tended to drift off me, he seemed to understand much of what I was saying.

"If anyone can find this guy, it's Batra," I said. "I've never seen anyone like her before."

John's eyes softened and he smiled. He tried to say something and couldn't. You could see how frustrating it was.

I put my hand on his shoulder and said, "You're in for a long haul, buddy, recovering from this. But if there's any man alive who can do it, you can."

Sampson's lazy, sad gaze came and dwelled around me for several seconds. Then he started struggling, as he got more and more upset.

"Hey," I said. "It's okay. We'll—"

Garbled sounds came out of his mouth.

He tried again. And again.

The sixth time, I thought he said, "Evan-widda."

"Evan-widda?" I said.

"Evan-widda…b…bag," he said, and then smiled and lifted his right hand to point to the surgical bandage. "Ho-ho…n…ed."

I frowned, but got it then, and smiled. "Even with a big hole in your head?"

Sampson smiled, dropped his hand, and winked at me before nodding off to sleep again, as if that had taken every bit of his strength.

But he'd spoken! Sort of. Definitely communicated. And the doctors had said his sense of humor could be gone with a wound to that part of his brain, but here he was making a joke about his situation.

If that wasn't a miracle, I don't know what is.

Billie arrived shortly before eight and beamed when I told her what had happened.

She kissed John, and said, "You spoke?"

He shook his head. "Alack vent…r…wrist…crist."

"What?"

"He said, 'Alex is a ventriloquist.' I think."

John grinned again and said, "Whips do no move."

Billie had tears in her eyes. "Lips don't move."

Sampson made a wheezing sound of delight that stayed with me on the way to work and buying a burner phone.

I went to Bree's office, and I knocked on her doorjamb.

"Long time no see," I said.

Bree glanced at the clock, said, "Are you getting obsessive about me?"

"I've always been obsessive about you, from the very first," I said.

"Liar," Bree said, but she was pleased.

"The truth," I said. "You had me the first time you glanced my way."

That pleased her even more. "Why are you buttering me up?"

"I'm not buttering you up," I said. "I was just flirting with my wife before I told her that Sampson spoke this morning."

"No?" she gasped. "He did?"

"It took a little interpretation, but he was telling jokes."

Bree got tears in her eyes, stood up, came around the desk, and hugged me. I got tears, too.

"Thanks," she said. "What a perfect thing to hear."

"I know," I said, before the cheap phone I'd bought on the way to work buzzed. Who knew the number? I'd just gotten the damn thing. Just activated it.

"Hello?" I said.

"It's Special Agent Batra."

"How'd you get this number?"

"By being good at my job," Agent Batra said, sounding annoyed. "I thought you'd be happy to hear from me so soon."

"I'm sorry," I said, though I was beginning to think there wasn't a box in the virtual universe that Henna Batra couldn't find and unlock if she set her mind to it. "You found something?"

"You were compromised in a troubling fashion."

I wanted to say that I could have told her that, but asked, "How so?"

"They got a bug into your son's computer operating system, piggybacked to a game app he downloaded at school."

"At his school?" I said, feeling queasy.

Soneji or The Soneji were not only threatening me in my house, they were targeting my youngest child.

"What else?" I demanded.

"Your daughter, Jannie, had the same bug in her system," Batra said. "It was uploaded to her computer without her knowledge when she was using her phone as a mobile hotspot at a coffee shop not far from your house."

This was worse. Both my children were being targeted.

"What about my phone? My wife's?" I asked, and turned on the speaker on the burner phone so Bree could hear.

"Clean," Batra said. "I'll have them messengered over in the next hour."

"Thank you," I said. "Is that it?"

"No, as a matter of fact," the FBI cyber expert said. "There was a similarity in the signature of the bug coder and the coder who created www.thesoneji.net."

I looked at Bree, who shrugged in confusion.

"You want to run that by us again?" I said.

The cybercrimes expert sounded irritated when she said, "Coders are artists in their own way, Detective. Just as classical painters had recognizable brushstrokes, great computer coders have a recognizable way of writing. Their signature, if you will."

"Makes sense," I said. "So who coded the website?"

Batra said, "It took me much, much longer than I expected to break through the firewalls that surrounded the identity of the creator and curator, but I did just a few minutes ago."

"Have you been up all night?" I asked.

"You said it was important."

Bree leaned forward, said, "Thank you, Agent Batra. It's Chief Stone here. Do you know who he is? The website creator?"

"She, and I've learned quite a bit about her in the past hour or so, thanks to a friend of mine at the NSA," Agent Batra said. "Especially the boyfriend she's fronting for. In fact, I know about him going right back to what his first-grade teacher said about him the day she recommended he be expelled from school."

I felt fear in the pit of my stomach. "And what was that?"

"She said she thought he was kind of a monster, Dr. Cross. Even then."

CHAPTER 26

AN HOUR LATER, I set in to wait on a bench in a hallway by the door to a loft space on the fourth floor of an older building off Dupont Circle.

I'd gotten into the building by showing my badge to a woman entering with groceries. I told her who I was looking for.

"Out running, that one," she'd replied. "Every lunch hour. Quite a sight."

I'd knocked on the door just in case, but there was no answer. I had a search warrant. I could have called for patrol to break the door down, but I hoped I could get more information by going patient and gentle.

Twenty minutes later, a fit Asian American woman in her late twenties came huffing up the staircase. Her black hair was cut short and her exposed arms were buff and sleeved in brilliantly colored tattoos.

Sweat poured down her face when she reached the landing and saw me getting off the bench. She didn't startle or try to escape as I'd expected.

Instead she hardened, said, "Took you a while, Dr. Cross. The intrusion was almost six hours ago. But here you are. At last. In the flesh."

"Kimiko Binx?" I said, holding up my badge and ID.

"Correct," Binx replied, walking toward me, palms held open at her sides, and studying me with great interest.

The closer she got, I noticed a device of some sort, orange, and strapped to her upper right arm. When I saw it blink, I thought *bomb,* and went for my gun.

"What's that on your arm?" I demanded, the pistol out, pointed her way.

Binx threw her hands up, said, "Whoa, whoa, Detective. It's a SPOT."

"What?"

"A GPS transmitter. It sends my position every thirty seconds to a satellite and to a website," she said. "I use it to track my running routes."

She turned sideways and held up her arm so I could examine the device. It was smaller than a smartphone, commercially made, heavy-duty plastic, with the SPOT logo emblazoned across the front of it and buttons with various icons. One said SOS and another was a shoe tread. The light blinked beside the shoe.

"So it tracks you?" I said.

"Correct," Binx said. "What do you want, Dr. Cross?"

I held the search warrant up and said, "If you could open the door."

Binx read the warrant without comment, fished out a key, and opened the loft. It was an airy work-and-living space with a view of an alley, a hodgepodge of used furniture, and a computer workstation that featured four large screens.

She moved toward the station.

"Do not go near your computer, Ms. Binx. Do not go near anything."

Binx got aggravated and took off the SPOT device. "You want this, too?"

"Please. Turn it off. Put it on the table there, and your phone if you've got it. I'd like to ask you some questions before I call for my evidence team."

"What do you want to know?" she asked, using her thumbs to play at the buttons on the transmitter.

"Why do you worship Gary Soneji?"

Binx didn't answer, hit one last button, and looked up at me before setting the SPOT on the table with the light no longer blinking.

"I don't worship Gary Soneji," she said finally. "I find Gary Soneji interesting. I find you interesting, for that matter."

"That why you built a high-security website about Soneji and me?"

"Yes," she said, sitting down calmly. "Other people find you two interesting also. Lots of them. It was a safe way to handle our common passion."

"Your members cheered when they found out my partner, John Sampson, was shot," I said.

"It's a private forum of free expression. I didn't approve of that."

"Didn't you?" I said angrily. "You provided space for sickos to plot terror in the name of a man who committed utterly heinous acts and died ten years ago."

"He's not dead," Binx said flatly. "Gary Soneji will never die."

I remembered the coffin coming up out of the ground in New Jersey, wondered how much longer the FBI's DNA testing would take, but said nothing of the exhumation of her idol.

Instead I said, "I don't get this, smart woman like you. Virginia Tech graduate. Write code for a living. Paid handsomely. Yet you get involved in something like this."

"Different strokes," she replied. "And it's my personal business."

"Not when it involves the shooting of a police officer. Nothing's personal."

"I had nothing to do with that, either," Binx said evenly. "Nothing. I'll take a lie detector."

"Who did, then?" I asked.

"Gary Soneji."

"Maybe," I said. "Or maybe Claude Watkins?"

Binx shifted her eyes ever so slightly to look just over my right shoulder before shaking her head.

I said, "Watkins's name is on your company's incorporation documents."

"Claude's a limited partner. He lent me some start-up money."

"Uh-huh," I said. "You know his background?"

"He had problems when he was younger," she said.

"He is a sadist, Ms. Binx. He was convicted of carving the skin off a little girl's fingers."

"He was chemically imbalanced back then," she said defiantly. "That was the diagnosis of both the state and his personal psychiatrists. He took the drugs they recommended, paid his dues, and moved on. Claude's a painter and performance artist now. He's brilliant."

"I'm sure he is," I said.

"No," Binx insisted. "He really is. I can take you to his studio. Show you. We've got nothing to hide. It's not far. He rents space in an old factory down by the Anacostia River, west bank."

"Address?"

She shrugged. "I just know how to get there.

I thought for a moment, said, "After my team gets here, you'll take me?"

She nodded. "Be glad to. Can I take a shower in the meantime? You can search the bathroom if you need to. I assure you it's nothing but the usual."

I stared at her for several beats, and then said, "Make it quick."

CHAPTER 27

THE CRIMINALISTS ARRIVED TEN minutes later. I was giving them instructions to call if they turned up anything when Kimiko Binx emerged from her bedroom in jeans, Nike running shoes, and a short-sleeved green blouse.

"Ready, Dr. Cross?" she said, coming toward me and then stumbling over a loose cord and losing her balance.

I reached out before she could fall. Binx grabbed onto my left hand and right forearm and got her balance.

She turned from me, looking back, puzzled. "What was that?"

"You should put your cords under rugs," I said. "Let's go."

We went downstairs to my car.

Binx got in the front seat, said, "Where's the siren?"

"It's not like that," I said. "Where am I going?"

"Toward the Anacostia Bridge. It's an old tool and die factory by the river."

I drove in silence until I realized she was studying me again.

"What are you looking at?"

"The object of Gary's obsession," she said.

"Soneji's sole obsession?" I asked.

"Well," Binx said, and turned to look out the windshield. "One of them."

She was so blithe and relaxed in her manner that I wondered if she was on some kind of medication. And yet, she made me feel strange, scrutinized by a cultist.

"How did you meet Claude Watkins?" I asked.

"At a party in Baltimore," she said. "Have you met him?"

"Haven't had the pleasure."

Binx smiled. "It is, you know. A pleasure to see his paintings and his performances."

"A real Picasso, then."

She caught the sarcasm, turned cooler, and said, "You'll see, Dr. Cross."

Binx navigated me toward a derelict light industrial area north of the bridge, and an abandoned brick-faced factory with a FOR SALE sign on the gate, which was unlocked.

"This is where the great painter and performance artist works?" I said.

"Correct," Binx said. "Claude moves around, takes month-to-month leases on abandoned buildings, where he's free to do his art without worrying about making a mess. When the building and the art's sold, he moves on. It's a win-win for everyone involved. He learned the tactic in Detroit."

It made sense, actually. I parked the car outside the gate, and felt odd, a little woozy, the way you do if you haven't eaten enough or stayed well hydrated. And my tongue felt thick, and my throat dry.

I heard Binx release her seat belt. It sounded louder than it should have. So did the key in the ignition beeping when I opened the door. I took the key out, stood up, felt the warm spring breeze, and felt almost immediately better.

I called up Google Maps on my phone, pinned my location, and texted the pin to Bree along with a message that said, "Send patrol for backup when you get the chance."

Then I drew my service weapon.

"Sorry to do this, Ms. Binx," I said. "But I need you in handcuffs."

"What? Why?"

"You're technically under arrest. I've just been a nice guy until now."

The computer coder didn't look happy as she came over. I got out my cuffs and buckled down her wrists, arms forward. She'd been cooperative for the most part and didn't seem much of a threat.

"What am I under arrest for?" Binx demanded. "Free speech?"

"How about fomenting and abetting attempted murder of a cop?"

"I did not!"

"You did," I said, pushing her in front of me.

We passed through the gate, crossed fifteen yards of scrub ground where purple crocuses poked out of weeds by a metal double door. Binx seemed on the verge of tears, opening one of the doors and saying, "I would never hurt a cop. My dad was a cop in Philly."

That surprised me. "Was?"

"He's retired," she said. "With a gold shield."

I looked at her differently now, the daughter of a good cop. Why would she get involved in something like this?

"You said you wanted to meet Claude," Binx said, trying to wipe her tears with her sleeves. "Let's go."

At first a voice in my head said not to enter the abandoned factory, to wait for backup, but then the voice was gone, replaced by a surge of clarity and confidence.

Keeping Binx squarely in front of me, I went inside.

Whenever you leave a sunny day for a darker quarter, there's always a fleeting moment when you're all but blind before your eyes adjust. It's also a time when you tend to be silhouetted in the doorway and are therefore an easy target.

But I heard no shot, and my vision refocused on a large, airy space, ten, maybe fifteen thousand square feet, with a ceiling that was warehouse-high and crisscrossed with rusted overhead tracks for heavy industrial lifts and booms.

Ten-foot-tall partitions carved the space up like a broad maze. The cement floor right in front of us was cracked, broken in places, and bare but for stacks of pipe and sheet metal, as if a reclaiming operation was under way. Thick dust hung in the air. Waves of it danced and swirled in the weak sunlight streaming through a bank of filthy windows high on the walls.

"I'm not seeing any paintings or studio," I said. "Where's Watkins?"

"He and the studio are in the back," Binx said, gesturing into the gloom. "I'll show you the way."

For the second time that day, that internal voice of mine, born of years of training and experience, raised doubts about following her until I had someone watching my back. And for the second time that day, I felt my heart beat faster, sensed more sharply my surroundings, and surged with another rush of complete confidence in my abilities.

"Lead on," I said, smiling at her, and feeling good, real good, like I was perfectly fine-tuned and ready for anything that might come my way.

Binx took me down one dim hallway, and then another, passing empty workroom after empty workroom before I smelled marijuana, fresh paint, and turpentine. The smells got stronger as we walked a short third hallway that dog-legged left and opened into a large, largely empty assembly-line room with dark alcoves off it on all four sides.

The only lights in the room were strong portable spots trained on one of several large paintings hanging on the far wall about fifty feet away. The painting showed a crane lifting a coffin from the ground. The headstone above the grave read "G. SONEJI." Two men stood by the grave. A Caucasian in a dark suit. And an African American in a blue police slicker. Me.

I almost smiled. Someone who'd been at the exhumation, probably Soneji or one of his followers, Watkins, had painted this, and yet I had to fight to keep from grinning at all the goodwill I felt inside.

*   *   *

The furthest of the three spotlights went dark then, revealing a man I couldn't see before because of the glare. He wore paint-speckled jeans, work boots, and a long-sleeved shirt, but his face was lost in shadows.

Then he took a step forward into a weak, dusty beam of sun-light coming through the grimy windows, revealing the wispy red hair and distinctive facial features of Gary Soneji.

"Dr. Cross," he said in a cracking, hoarse voice. "I thought you'd never catch up."

CHAPTER 28

SONEJI MOVED HIS ARM then, and I saw the gun he held at his side, a nickel-plated pistol, just like the ones he used to shoot Sampson and me.

Take him!

The voice screamed in my head, ending all of those strange good feelings that had been inexplicably surging through me.

I raised my service pistol fast, pushed Binx out of the way, aimed at Soneji, and shouted, "Drop your weapon now or I'll shoot!"

To my surprise, Soneji let go the gun. It fell to the floor with a clatter. He raised his hands, studying me calmly and with great interest.

"Facedown on the floor!" I shouted. "Hands behind your back!"

Soneji started to follow my orders before Binx hit my gun hand with both her fists. The blow knocked me off balance, and my gun discharged just as a spotlight went on from above the paintings, blinding me.

There was a shot.

Then all the lights died, leaving me disoriented, and blinking at dazzling blue spots that danced before my eyes. Knowing I was vulnerable, I threw myself to the floor, expecting another shot at any moment.

It was a trap. The whole thing was a trap, and I'd just walked into…

The spots cleared.

Soneji was gone. So was Binx. And Soneji's nickel-plated pistol.

I held my position, and peered around, noticing for the first time a metal table covered in cans of paint and paintbrushes. And then those alcoves all around the room. They were low-roofed and dark with shadows.

Soneji and Binx could easily have slid into one of them. And what? Escaped? Or were they just waiting for me to make a move?

I had no answers, and stayed where I was, listening, looking.

Nothing moved. And there was zero sound.

But I could feel him there. Soneji. Listening for me. Looking for me.

I felt severely agitated at those ideas, almost wired before an irrational, all-consuming rage erupted inside me. Standard protocol was gone, burned up. All my training was gone, too, consumed by the flames of wanting to take Gary Soneji down. Now and for good.

I lurched to my feet and ran hard at the nearest alcove on the opposite wall. Every nerve expected a shot, but there was none. I got to the protection of the alcove, gasping, gun up, seeing the remnants of machine tools.

But no Soneji.

"I've got backup, Gary," I shouted. "They're surrounding the place!"

No response. Were they gone?

I dodged out of the alcove and moved fast along the wall to the next anteroom, the one directly beneath the painting of the exhumation. At first I saw only large rolls of canvas laid on sawhorses and tables made of plywood.

Then, in the deepest shadows of the alcove, and in my peripheral vision, I caught a flash of movement. I spun left to see Soneji stooping forward on the balls of his feet as he took two halting steps, and straightened up.

His mouth opened as if in anticipation of some long-awaited pleasure. His gun hand started to rise.

I shot him twice, the deafening reports making my ears buzz and ring like they'd been boxed hard. Gary Soneji jerked twice, and screamed like a woman before staggering and falling from sight.

CHAPTER 29

MY HEART BOOMED IN my chest, but my brain sighed with relief.

Soneji was hit hard. He was crying, dying there on the canvas-room floor where I couldn't see him.

My pistol still up, I took an uncertain step toward Soneji, and another. A third and fourth step and I saw him lying there, no gun in his hand or around him, looking at me with a piteous expression.

In a high, whimpering voice, he said, "Why did you shoot me? Why me?"

Before I could answer, Soneji went into a coughing fit that turned wet and choking. Then blood streamed from his lips, his eyes started to dull, and the life went out of him with a last hard breath.

"Oh, my God!" Binx screamed behind me. "What have you done?"

"Soneji's gone," I said, feeling intense, irrational pleasure course through me. "He's finally gone."

Binx was crying. I started to turn toward her. She saw the gun in my hand, turned terrified, and leaped out of sight.

Binx had led me into a trap, I thought. Binx had led me here to die.

I ran after her into the main room, saw her running crazily back the way we'd come in, and heard her making these petrified whining sounds.

"Stop, Ms. Binx!" I yelled after her.

As I did, I caught a shift in the shadows of an alcove at the far end of the room. I looked toward it, shocked to see that beyond two fifty-five-gallon drums, Gary Soneji stood there in the mouth of the alcove, same clothes, same hair, same face, same nickel-plated pistol in hand.

How was that…?

Before I could shake off the shock of there being two Sonejis, he fired at me. His bullet pinged off the post of one of those spotlights trained on the paintings. On instinct, I threw myself toward him, gun up and firing.

My first shot was wide, but my next one spun the second Soneji around just before I landed hard on the cement floor. Doubled over, he went down too, gasping, groaning, and trying to crawl back into the alcove.

I scrambled to my feet, and charged his position. A spotlight went on above the alcove, trying to strike me in the eyes again. But I got my free hand up before it could blind me.

From high and to my right, a gun went off. The bullet blew a chunk of cement out of the floor at my feet.

I dove behind the fifty-five-gallon drums, glanced at the second Soneji, who was still crawling, and leaving a trail of dark blood behind him.

The voice in my head screamed at me to use my phone and call it in. I needed sirens coming now.

Then I heard the sirens, distant but distinct, before another gunshot sounded from up high and to my right again. It smacked the near barrel, the slug making a clanging noise as it ricocheted inside.

I winced, rolled over, and peered up through the narrow gap between the barrels, seeing a third Gary Soneji standing on the roof of the alcove above the exhumation painting. He was trying to aim at me with a nickel-plated pistol.

Before he could fire, I did.

The third Soneji screamed, dropped his gun, and grabbed at his thigh before toppling off the roof. He fell a solid ten feet, hit the cement floor hard enough to make cracking sounds. He screamed feebly, then lay there moaning.

I stood up then, shaking with adrenaline, and feeling that beautiful rage explode through me all over again, searing-hot and vengeful.

"Who's next?" I roared, feeling almost giddy. "C'mon, you bastards! I'll kill every single Soneji before I'm done!"

I swung all around, my pistol aiming high and low, finger twitching on the trigger, anticipating another Soneji to appear on the roof of the alcove or from the darkness of the three remaining anterooms.

But nothing moved, and there was no sound except for the moans of the wounded and of Kimiko Binx, who sat in the far corner of the main room, curled up in a fetal position, and sobbing.

CHAPTER 30

KIMIKO BINX WAS STILL crying and refusing to talk to me or to the patrol officers who arrived first on the scene, or to the detectives who came soon after.

Not even Bree could get Binx to make any kind of statement, other than to say sullenly, "Cross didn't have to shoot. He didn't have to kill them all."

The fact was, I had not killed them all. Two of the Sonejis were alive, and there were EMTs working feverishly on them.

"Three Sonejis?" Bree said. "Makes it easy for them to cover ground."

I nodded, seeing how one of them could have shot Sampson, while another staked out Soneji's grave, and the third could have driven by Bree and me outside GW Medical Center.

"You okay, Alex?" Bree asked.

"No," I said, feeling incredibly tired all of a sudden. "Not really."

"Tell me what happened," Bree said.

I did to the best of my abilities, finishing with "But all you really need to know is they set up an ambush, lured me, and I walked right into it."

Bree thought about that, and then said, "There'll be an investigation, but from what you said, it's cut-and-dry. Self-defense, and justified."

I didn't say anything because somehow it didn't seem quite right to me. Justified, yes, but cut-and-dry? They'd tried to kill Sampson, and me, twice. But some of the threads of what had happened just didn't—

"By the way," Bree said, interrupting my thoughts. "The labs came back on the exhumation."

I looked at her, revealing nothing. "And?"

"It was him in the coffin," she said. "Soneji. They compared DNA to samples taken when he was in federal custody the first time. He's dead, Alex. He's been dead more than ten years."

One of the EMTs called out to us before I could express my relief. We went to the Soneji in the far alcove, then the one who'd been crawling away, leaving blood like a snail's track. They'd shot him up with morphine and he was out of it. They'd also cut off his shirt and found the raised latex edge of a mask that could have been crafted by one of Hollywood's finest.

After photographing the mask, we sliced and peeled it off, revealing the ashen face of Claude Watkins, painter, performance artist, and wounded idolizer of Gary Soneji.

The second Soneji was up on a gurney and headed for an ambulance when we caught up to him.

We tore open his shirt, found the latex edge of an identical mask, photographed it, and then had the EMTs slice it off him. The man behind the mask was in his late twenties and unfamiliar to us. But as they wheeled him out, I had no doubt that, whoever he was, he'd been worshipping Gary Soneji for a long, long time.

We waited for the medical examiner to arrive and take custody of the dead Soneji before we cut off the third mask.

"It's a woman," Bree said, her hands going to her mouth.

"Not just any woman," I said, stunned and confused. "That's Virginia Winslow."

"Who?"

"Gary Soneji's widow."

"Wait. What?" Bree said, staring at the dead woman closely. "I thought you said she hated Soneji."

"That's what she told me."

Bree shook her head. "What in God's name possessed her to impersonate her dead husband and then try to kill you? Did she shoot John? Or did Watkins? Or that other guy?"

"One of them did," I said. "I'll put money one of the pistols matches."

"But why?" she said, still confused.

"Binx and Watkins and, evidently, Virginia Winslow made Soneji into a cult, with me being the enemy of the cult," I said, and thought about Winslow's son, Dylan, and the picture of me on his dartboard.

Where was the kid in all of this? Seeing Binx being led out, I thought that if we leaned on her hard enough, she'd eventually want to cut a deal and tell all.

"You look like hell, you know," Bree said, breaking my thoughts again.

"Appreciate the compliment."

"I'm serious. Let's go, let the crime-scene guys do their work."

"No formal statement?"

"You've made enough of a statement to satisfy me for the time being."

"Chief of detectives and wife," I said. "That's a conflict of interest any way you look at it."

"I don't care, Alex," Bree said. "I'm taking you home. You can make a formal statement after you've had a good night's sleep."

I almost agreed, but then said, "Okay, I'll leave. But can we stop by Sampson's room before we go home? He deserves to know."

"Of course," she said, softening. "Of course we can."

I stayed quiet during the ride away from the ambush and shooting scene. Bree seemed to understand I needed space, and didn't ask any more questions on the way to GW Medical Center.

But my mind kept jumping to different aspects of the case. Where had Watkins and Soneji's widow met? Through Kimiko Binx? And who was the other wounded guy? How had he come to be part of a conspiracy to kill me and Sampson?

Riding the elevator to the ICU, I promised myself I'd answer the questions, clean up the case, even though it was all but over.

As the door opened, I felt something sharp on my right arm and jerked back to look at it.

"Sorry," Bree said. "You had a little piece of Scotch tape there."

She showed me the tape, no more than a half inch long, before rolling it between her thumb and index finger and flicking it into a trash can.

I twisted my forearm, to see a little reddish patch, and wondered where I'd picked that up. Probably off Nana Mama's counter earlier in the morning, left over from one of Ali's latest school projects.

It didn't matter because when we reached the ICU, the nurse gave us good news. Sampson was gone, transferred to the rehab floor.

When we finally tracked him down, he was paying his first visit to the physical therapist's room. We went in and found Billie with her palms pressed to her beaming cheeks, and her eyes welling over with tears.

I had to fight back tears, too.

Sampson was not only out of bed, he was out of a wheelchair, up on his feet, with his back to us, using a set of parallel gymnastics bars for balance. His massive arm and neck muscles were straining so hard they were trembling, and sweat gushed off him as he moved one foot and then the other, a drag more than a step with his right leg. But it was incredible.

"Can you believe it?" Billie cried, jumped to her feet, and hugged Bree.

I wiped at my tears, kissed Billie, and broke into a huge grin before clapping and coming around in front of Sampson.

Big John had a hundred-watt smile going.

He saw me, stopped, and said, " 'Ow bout that?"

"Amazing," I said, fighting back more emotion. "Just amazing, brother."

He smiled broader, and then cocked his head at me, as if he felt something.

"Wha?" Sampson said.

"I got him," I said. "The one who shot you."

Sampson sobered, and paused to take that in. The therapist offered him the wheelchair, but he shook his head slowly, still staring at me intently, as if seeing all sorts of things in my face.

"F-get him f-now, Alex," John said finally, with barely a slur and his face twisting into a triumphant smile. "Can't yah see I got dance less. . .sons ta do?"

I stood there in shock for a moment. Bree and Billie started laughing. So did Sampson and the therapist.

I did, too, then, from deep in my gut, a belly laughter that soon mixed with deep and profound gratitude, and a great deal of awe.

Our prayers had been answered. A true miracle had occurred.

My partner and best friend had been shot in the head, but Big John Sampson was not defeated and definitely on his way back.

EPILOGUE

TWO DAYS LATER, I awoke feeling strangely out of it, as if I were nursing the last dregs of the worst hangover of my life.

Department protocol dictated I sit on the sidelines on paid administrative leave while the shootings were investigated. After what I'd been through, and because I was feeling so run-down, I should have taken the time to stay home and recover with my family for at least a week.

But I forced myself out of bed and headed downtown to talk with my union representative, a sharp attorney named Carrie Nan. I walked her through the events in the factory. Like Bree, she felt comfortable with me talking to Internal Affairs, which I did.

The two detectives, Alice Walker and Gary Pan, were polite, thorough, and, I thought, fair. They took me through the scenario six or seven times in an interrogation room I'd used often on the job.

I stuck with the facts, and not the swinging emotions of elation and rage that I'd felt during the entire event. I kept it clean and to the point.

The scene was an ambush. In all three shootings, I'd seen a pistol. I'd made a warning. When the pistol was turned on me, I shot to save my life.

Detective Pan scratched his head. "You sound kind of detached when you describe what happened."

"Do I?" I said. "I'm just trying to talk about it objectively."

"Always said you were the sharpest tack around, Dr. Cross," Detective Walker said, and then paused. "After you shot the third Soneji, did you scream something like 'I'll kill every single Soneji before I'm through?'"

I remembered, and it sounded bad, and I knew it.

"They had me surrounded," I said at last. "I was caught in an ambush, and had already engaged with three of them. Did I lose my cool at that point? I might have. But it was over by then. If there were others, they were long gone."

Pan said, "Kimiko Binx was there."

"Yes. What's she saying?"

Walker said, "We're not at liberty to say, Dr. Cross, you know that."

"Sure," I said. "Just being nosy."

Pan said, "There *were* others there, by the way. In the factory."

Before I could say anything, Pan's cell buzzed. Then Walker's.

"What others?" I asked. "I didn't see anyone else."

The detectives read their texts, and didn't answer me.

"Sit tight," Pan said, getting up.

"You need anything?" Walker asked. "Coffee? Coke?"

"Just water," I said, and watched them leave.

There were others there, by the way. In the factory.

I hadn't seen a soul. But was that true? Different spotlights had been aimed at me from different places and angles. There had to have been a fifth person at the least. There had to—

Two men in suits entered the room along with Chief Michaels and Bree. The first three were stone-faced. Bree looked like she was on the edge of a breakdown.

"I'm sorry, Alex, but…," she said, barely getting the words out before she looked to Chief Michaels. "I can't."

"Can't what?" I asked, feeling as if I were suddenly standing with my back to the rim of a deep canyon I hadn't even realized was there.

"Alex," Michaels said. "The third Soneji, the one you shot off the roof of the alcove, died two hours ago. And some very damning information has come forward that directly contradicts your account of the shooting."

"What evidence?" I said. "Who are these guys?"

One of the suits said, "Mr. Cross, I am Special Agent Carlos Ramon with the US Justice Department."

Coming around the table, the other suit said, "Special Agent Jon Christopher, Justice. You are under arrest for the premeditated murder of Virginia Winslow and John Doe. You have the right to remain silent. Anything you say can and—"

I didn't hear the rest. I didn't need to. I'd recited the Miranda warnings a thousand times. As they handcuffed me, I kept looking at Bree, who was crushed, and wouldn't return my gaze.

"You don't believe them, do you?" I said, as Pan started to urge me toward the door and booking. "Bree?"

Bree looked my way finally with devastated, teary eyes. "Don't say another word, Alex. Everything can and will be used against you now."

"I'M NOT ON TRIAL. SAN FRANCISCO IS."

Drug cartel boss the Kingfisher has a reputation for being violent
and merciless. And after he's finally caught, he's set to stand trial
for his vicious crimes—until he begins unleashing chaos and terror upon the lawyers, jurors, and police associated with the case.
The city is paralyzed, and Detective Lindsay Boxer is caught in
the eye of the storm.

Will the Women's Murder Club make it out alive—or will a
courtroom shocker ensure their last breaths?

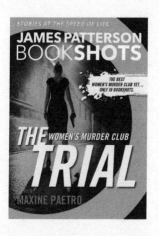

**Read on for a sneak peek at the shocking new
Women's Murder Club story.
Coming soon from**

BOOKSHOTS

IT WAS THAT CRAZY period between Thanksgiving and Christmas when work overflowed, time raced, and there wasn't enough light between dawn and dusk to get everything done.

Still, our gang of four, what we call the Women's Murder Club, always had a spouse-free holiday get-together dinner of drinks and bar food.

Yuki had picked the place.

It was called Uncle Maxie's Top Hat and was a bar and grill that had been a fixture in the Financial District for 150 years. It was decked out with art deco prints and mirrors on the walls, and a large, neon-lit clock behind the bar dominated the room. Maxie's catered to men in smart suits and women in tight skirts and spike heels who wore good jewelry.

I liked the place and felt at home there in a Mickey Spillane kind of way. Case in point: I was wearing straight-legged pants, a blue gabardine blazer, a Glock in my shoulder holster, and flat lace-up shoes. I stood in the bar area, slowly turning my head as I looked around for my BFFs.

"Lindsay. Yo."

Cindy waved her hand from the table tucked under the spiral staircase. I waved back, moved toward the nook inside the cranny.

Claire was wearing a trench coat over her scrubs, with a button on the lapel that read SUPPORT OUR TROOPS. She peeled off her coat and gave me a hug and a half.

Cindy was also in her work clothes: cords and a bulky sweater, with a peacoat slung over the back of her chair. If I'd ducked under the table, I'm sure I would have seen steel-toed boots. Cindy is a crime reporter of note, and she was wearing her on-the-job hound dog clothes.

She blew me a couple of kisses, and Yuki stood up to give me her seat and a jasmine-scented smack on the cheek. She had clearly come from court, where she worked as a pro bono defense attorney for the poor and hopeless. Still, she was dressed impeccably, in pinstripes and pearls.

I took the chair across from Claire. She sat between Cindy and Yuki with her back to the room, and we all scooched up to the smallish glass-and-chrome table.

If it hasn't been said, we four are a mutual heart, soul, and work society in which we share our cases and views of the legal system, as well as our personal lives. Right now the girls were worried about me.

Three of us were married: me, Claire, and Yuki; and Cindy had a standing offer of a ring and vows to be exchanged in Grace Cathedral. Until very recently you couldn't have found four more happily hooked-up women. Then the bottom fell out of my marriage to Joe Molinari, the father of my child and a man I shared everything with, including my secrets.

We had had it so good, we kissed and made up before our fights were over. It was the typical: "You are right." "No, you are!"

Then Joe went missing during possibly the worst weeks of my life.

I'm a homicide cop, and I know when someone is telling me the truth and when things do not add up.

Joe missing in action had not added up. Because of that I had worried almost to panic. Where was he? Why hadn't he checked in? Why were my calls bouncing off his full mailbox? Was he still alive?

As the crisscrossed threads of espionage, destruction, and mass murder were untangled, Joe finally made his curtain call with stories of his past and present lives that I'd never heard before. I found plenty of reason not to trust him anymore.

Even he would agree. I think anyone would.

It's not news that once trust is broken, it's damned hard to superglue it back together. And for me it might take more time and belief in Joe's confession than I actually had.

I still loved him. We'd shared a meal when he came to see our baby, Julie. We didn't make any moves toward getting divorced that night, but we didn't make love, either. Our relationship was now like the Cold War in the eighties between Russia and the USA, a strained but practical peace called détente.

Now, as I sat with my friends, I tried to put Joe out of my mind, safe in the knowledge that my nanny was looking after Julie and that the home front was safe. I ordered a favorite holiday drink, a hot buttered rum, and a rare steak sandwich with Uncle Maxie's hot chili sauce.

My girlfriends were deep in criminal cross talk about Claire's holiday overload of corpses, Cindy's new cold case she'd exhumed from the *San Francisco Chronicle*'s dead letter files, and Yuki's hoped-for favorable verdict for her client, an underage drug dealer. I was almost caught up when Yuki said, "Linds, I gotta ask. Any Christmas plans with Joe?"

And that's when I was saved by the bell. My phone rang.

My friends said in unison, "NO PHONES."

It was the rule, but I'd forgotten—again.

I reached into my bag for my phone, saying, "Look, I'm turning it off."

But I saw that the call was from Rich Conklin, my partner and Cindy's fiancé. She recognized his ring tone on my phone.

"There goes our party," she said, tossing her napkin into the air.

"Linds?" said Conklin.

"Rich, can this wait? I'm in the middle—"

"It's Kingfisher. He's in a shoot-out with cops at the Vault. There've been casualties."

"But—Kingfisher is *dead*."

"Apparently, he's returned from the grave."

MY PARTNER WAS DOUBLE-PARKED and waiting for me outside Uncle Maxie's, with the engine running and the flashers on. I got into the passenger seat of the unmarked car, and Richie handed me my vest. He's that way, like a younger version of a big brother. He thinks of me, watches out for me, and I try to do the same for him.

He watched me buckle up, then he hit the sirens and stepped on the gas.

We were about five minutes from the Vault, a class A nightclub on the second floor of a former Bank of America building.

"Fill me in," I said to my partner.

"Call came in to 911 about ten minutes ago," Conklin said as we tore up California Street. "A kitchen worker said he recognized Kingfisher out in the bar. He was still trying to convince 911 that it was an emergency when shots were fired inside the club."

"Watch out on our right."

Richie yanked the wheel hard left to avoid an indecisive panel truck, then jerked it hard right and took a turn onto Sansome.

"You okay?" he asked.

I had been known to get carsick in jerky high-speed chases when I wasn't behind the wheel.

"I'm fine. Keep talking."

My partner told me that a second witness reported to first officers that three men were talking to two women at the bar. One of the men yelled, "No one screws with the King." Shots were fired. The women were killed.

"Caller didn't leave his name."

I was gripping both the dash and the door, and had both feet on imaginary brakes, but my mind was occupied with Kingfisher. He was a Mexican drug cartel boss, a psycho with a history of brutality and revenge, and a penchant for settling his scores personally.

Richie was saying, "Patrol units arrived as the shooters were attempting to flee through the front entrance. Someone saw the tattoo on the back of the hand of one of the shooters. I talked to Brady," Conklin said, referring to our lieutenant. "If that shooter is Kingfisher and survives, he's ours."

I WANTED THE KING on death row for the normal reasons. He was to the drug and murder trade as al-Baghdadi was to terrorism. But I also had personal reasons.

Earlier that year a cadre of dirty San Francisco cops from our division had taken down a number of drug houses for their own financial gain. One drug house in particular yielded a payoff of five to seven million in cash and drugs. Whether those cops knew it beforehand or not, the stolen loot belonged to Kingfisher—and he wanted it back.

The King took his revenge but was still short a big pile of dope and dollars.

So he turned his sights on me.

I was the primary homicide inspector on the dirty-cop case.

Using his own twisted logic, the King demanded that I personally recover and return his property. Or else.

It was a threat and a promise, and of course I couldn't deliver.

From that moment on I had protection all day and night, every day and night, but protection isn't enough when your tormentor is like a ghost. We had grainy photos and shoddy footage from cheap surveillance cameras on file. We had a blurry picture of a tattoo on the back of his left hand.

That was all.

After his threat I couldn't cross the street from my apartment to my car without fear that Kingfisher would drop me dead in the street.

A week after the first of many threatening phone calls, the calls stopped. A report came in from the Mexican federal police saying that they had turned up the King's body in a shallow grave in Baja. That's what they said.

I had wondered then if the King was really dead. If the freaking nightmare was truly over.

I had just about convinced myself that my family and I were safe. Now the breaking news confirmed that my gut reaction had been right. Either the Mexican police had lied, or the King had tricked them with a dead doppelganger buried in the sand.

A few minutes ago the King had been identified by a kitchen worker at the Vault. If true, why had he surfaced again in San Francisco? Why had he chosen to show his face in a nightclub filled with people? Why shoot two women inside that club? And my number one question: Could we bring him in alive and take him to trial?

Please, God. Please.

OUR CAR RADIO WAS barking, crackling, and squealing at a high pitch as cars were directed to the Vault, in the middle of the block on Walnut Street. Cruisers and ambulances screamed past us as Conklin and I closed in on the scene. I badged the cop at the perimeter, and immediately after, Rich backed our car into a gap in the pack of law enforcement vehicles, parking it across the street from the Vault.

The Vault was built of stone block. It had two centered large glass doors, now shattered, with a half-circular window across the doorframe. Flanking the doors were two tall windows, capped with demilune windows, glass also shot out.

Shooters inside the Vault were using the granite doorframe as a barricade as they leaned out and fired on the uniformed officers positioned behind their car doors.

Conklin and I got out of our car with our guns drawn and crouched beside our wheel wells. Adrenaline whipped my heart into a gallop. I watched everything with clear eyes, and yet my mind flooded with memories of past shoot-outs. I had been shot and almost died. All three of my partners had been shot, one of them fatally.

And now I had a baby at home.

A cop at the car to my left shouted, *"Christ!"*

Her gun spun out of her hand and she grabbed her shoulder as she dropped to the asphalt. Her partner ran to her, dragged her toward the rear of the car, and called in, "Officer down." Just then SWAT arrived in force with a small caravan of SUVs and a ballistic armored transport vehicle as big as a bus. The SWAT commander used his megaphone, calling to the shooters, who had slipped back behind the fortresslike walls of the Vault.

"All exits are blocked. There's nowhere to run, nowhere to hide. Toss out the guns, now."

The answer to the SWAT commander was a fusillade of gunfire that pinged against steel chassis. SWAT hit back with automatic weapons, and two men fell out of the doorway onto the pavement.

The shooting stopped, leaving an echoing silence.

The commander used his megaphone and called out, "You. Put your gun down and we won't shoot. Fair warning. We're coming in."

"WAIT. I give up," said an accented voice. "Hands up, see?"

"Come all the way out. Come to me," said the SWAT commander.

I could see him from where I stood.

The last of the shooters was a short man with a café au lait complexion, a prominent nose, dark hair that was brushed back. He was wearing a well-cut suit that had blood splatted on the white shirt as he came out through the doorway with his hands up.

Two guys in tactical gear grabbed him and slammed him over the hood of an SUV, then cuffed and arrested him.

The SWAT commander dismounted from the armored vehicle.

I recognized him as Reg Covington. We'd worked together before. Conklin and I walked over to where Reg was standing beside the last of the shooters.

Covington said, "Boxer. Conklin. You know this guy?"

He stood the shooter up so I could get a good look at his face. I'd never met Kingfisher. I compared the real-life suspect with my memory of the fuzzy videos I'd seen of Jorge Sierra, a.k.a. the King.

"Let me see his hands," I said.

It was a miracle that my voice sounded steady, even to my own ears. I was sweating and my breathing was shallow. My gut told me that this was the man.

Covington twisted the prisoner's hands so that I could see the backs of them. On the suspect's left hand was the tattoo of a kingfisher, the same as the one in the photo in Kingfisher's slim file.

I said to our prisoner, "Mr. Sierra. I'm Sergeant Boxer. Do you need medical attention?"

"Mouth-to-mouth resuscitation, maybe."

Covington jerked him to his feet and said, "We'll take good care of him. Don't worry."

He marched the King to the waiting paddy wagon, and I watched as he was shackled and chained to the bar before the door was closed.

Covington slapped the side of the van, and it took off as CSI and the medical examiner's van moved in and SWAT thundered into the Vault to clear the scene.

ABOUT THE AUTHOR

JAMES PATTERSON has written more bestsellers and created more enduring fictional characters than any other novelist writing today. He lives in Florida with his family.

MICHAEL BENNETT FACES HIS TOUGHEST CASE YET....

Detective Michael Bennett is called to the scene after a man plunges to his death outside a trendy Manhattan hotel— but the man's fingerprints are traced to a pilot who was killed in Iraq years ago.

Will Bennett discover the truth?

Or will he become tangled in a web of government secrets?

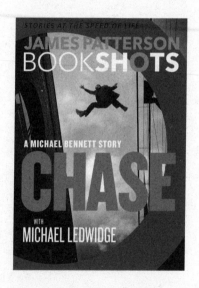

Read the new action-packed Michael Bennett story, *Chase*, coming soon from

BOOK**SHOTS**

SOME GAMES AREN'T FOR CHILDREN....

After a nasty divorce, Christy Moore finds her escape in Marty Hawking who introduces her to all sorts of new experiences, including an explosive new game called "Make-Believe." But what begins as innocent fun soon turns dark, and as Marty pushes the boundaries further and further, the game may just end up deadly.

Read the white-knuckle thriller, coming soon from

BOOKSHOTS

CAN A LITTLE BLACK DRESS CHANGE EVERYTHING?

Divorced magazine editor Jane Avery is content with spending her nights alone—until she finds *The Dress*. Suddenly she's surrendering to dark desires, and New York City has become her erotic playground. But what begins as a sultry fantasy has gone too far....
And her next conquest could be her last.

Check out the steamy cliffhanger *Little Black Dress,* coming soon from

BOOK**SHOTS**

LOOKING TO FALL IN LOVE IN JUST ONE NIGHT?

INTRODUCING BOOKSHOTS FLAMES:
original romances presented by James Patterson that fit into your busy life.

FEATURING LOVE STORIES BY:

New York Times bestselling author Jen McLaughlin
New York Times bestselling author Samantha Towle
USA Today bestselling author Erin Knightley
Elizabeth Hayley
Jessica Linden
Codi Gary
Laurie Horowitz
…and many others!

COMING SOON FROM

SHE NEVER EXPECTED TO FALL IN LOVE WITH A COWBOY....

Rodeo king Tanner Callen isn't looking to be tied down anytime soon. When he sees Madeline Harper at a local honky-tonk— even though everything about her screams New York City—he brings out every trick in his playbook to take her home. But soon he learns that he doesn't just want her for a night. Instead, he hopes for forever.

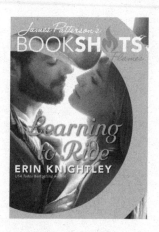

Read the heartwarming new romance *Learning to Ride*, coming soon from

HER SECOND CHANCE AT LOVE MIGHT BE TOO GOOD TO BE TRUE....

When Chelsea O'Kane escapes to her family's inn in Maine, all she's got are fresh bruises, a gun in her lap, and a desire to start anew. That's when she runs into her old flame, Jeremy Holland. As he helps her fix up the inn, they rediscover what they once loved about each other.

Until it seems too good to last...

Read the stirring story of hope and redemption
The McCullagh Inn in Maine, **coming soon from**